THE WEDDING

Other novels by Gurjinder Basran

Everything Was Good-bye

Someone You Love is Gone

Help! I'm Alive

GURJINDER BASRAN

THE WEDDING

a novel

Douglas & McIntyre

Douglas and McIntyre (2013) Ltd.
P.O. Box 219, Madeira Park, BC, V0N 2H0
www.douglas-mcintyre.com

Edited by Karlene Nicolajsen
Cover design by Anna Comfort O'Keeffe and Christine Mangosing
Text design by Libris Simas Ferraz/Onça Publishing
Printed and bound in Canada

Douglas and McIntyre acknowledges the support of the Canada Council for the Arts, the Government of Canada, and the Province of British Columbia through the BC Arts Council.

Library and Archives Canada Cataloguing in Publication
Title: The wedding : a novel / Gurjinder Basran.
Names: Basran, Gurjinder, author.
Identifiers: Canadiana (print) 20240404289 | Canadiana (ebook) 20240404351
     | ISBN 9781771624169 (softcover) | ISBN 9781771624176 (EPUB)
Classification: LCC PS8603.A789 W43 2024 | DDC C813/.6—dc23

For my family

"Know your own happiness. You want nothing but patience—
or give it a more fascinating name, call it hope."

—JANE AUSTEN

TABLE OF CONTENTS

Characters · viii

You're Invited! · x

Vadayaan · 1

Dear Auntie · 17

Basic Baby · 28

No Thru Road · 47

Ready for This Jelly? · 60

Best Laid Plans · 75

Mottu · 83

Just the Best of Us · 105

How I Wonder Who You Are · 116

A Gaggle, a Mischief, a Murder · 127

Love Languages · 141

Lucky, Lucky Boy · 148

You Indians Are Everywhere · 156

A Good Family · 166

The Brampton Bride's Advice · 172

Cold Feet · 181

God Willing · 186

Izzat · 194

The Morning After · 198

Epilogue · 208

Acknowledgements · 210

About the Author · 211

CHARACTERS

Dosanjh Family and Guests

Devinder "Devi" Dosanjh .... Bride

Gurjot "Jot" Dosanjh .... Brother of the bride

Bhajan Dosanjh .... Father of the bride

Ramandeep "Raman" Dosanjh .... Mother of the bride

Darshan Dosanjh .... Paternal grandmother (Dadi) of the bride

Seva Dosanjh .... Paternal grandfather of the bride

Jasvir Sidhu .... Great-aunt (Bhua) of the bride

Jessie Bhatti .... Childhood friend of Gurjot

Atwal Family and Guests

Nanak "Baby" Atwal .... Groom
Gobind "Gobi" Atwal .... Brother of the groom
Satnam Atwal .... Father of the groom
Balbir Atwal .... Mother of the groom
Sonia "Mottu" Nijjar .... Family friend
Veero "Boston Auntie" Nijjar ..... Family friend; mother of Sonia
Gurmaan Nijjar .... Family friend; father of Sonia
Margaret Richardson .... Neighbour

Event Staff

Priya Deol .... Local journalist
Jag .... Bride's stylist and makeup artist
Rish, "Rishee" .... Wedding photographer
Twinkle .... Kitchen staff at Goldie's Palace

YOU'RE INVITED!

Sangeet Ceremony
June 28, 2022

Mehndi Party
June 30, 2022

Maiyan
July 1, 2022

Wedding
July 2, 2022

Reception
July 2, 2022

EK JOT DOYE MURTI

They are not said to be husband and wife who merely
sit together. Rather they alone are called husband
and wife who have one soul in two bodies.

— GURU AMAR DAS

Mr. Bhajan Singh Dosanjh
and
Mrs. Ramandeep Kaur Dosanjh
request the pleasure of your company on the auspicious
occasion of the wedding ceremony of their beloved daughter

Devinder

(granddaughter of Sardar Seva Singh and
Sardarni Darshan Kaur Dosanjh)

with

Nanak

(son of Satnam Singh Atwal and Balbir Kaur Atwal)

on Saturday, the second of July, two thousand and twenty-two
at
Nanaksar Gurdwara Gursikh Temple
10 King Road, Vancouver, BC

Arrival of Baraat	9:30 a.m.
Milini and Tea	10:00 a.m.
Anand Karaj	11:00 a.m.
Guru ka Langar	12:00 p.m.

Best compliments from all friends and relatives.
No gifts please.

VADAYAAN

JASVIR PEERED THROUGH THE LIVING ROOM SHEERS, WATCHING HER sister-in-law struggle to get out of the shiny black car. Darshan had not just shrunk, as people do with age, she had collapsed in on herself, hunched forward on a cane, her round body shifting from side to side as if she were walking slowly over hot coals, her weeble-wobble movements setting the pace for her son and his wife, whose ardent offers to help her up the stairs were declined with a dismissive gesture. As they came closer to the front door, Jasvir turned away from the window, closed her eyes tight as if she could wish them away. She listened to them comment on the Sold sign planted in her front lawn, their curious voices soon drowned out by the sound of the elaborate doorbell her late husband, Dalbir, had loved so much. She remembered how proud he was when they built the house, how he took friends and family on a tour of the not-yet fully framed rooms, how it smelled like timber and metal and how that smell still made her nostalgic. "Picture it," he'd said as he panned the air with his hands, but somehow she could never quite imagine it.

As the Westminster bell chimed, she wondered what to do. She knew why they were here. Earlier in the day, her cousin had called to say they'd just been to her house to deliver the invitation, and in doing so she had shared whatever new gossip there was about the groom and his family, and rehashed the sordid details around the shooting that had left his older brother paralyzed. "Suchee," was all Jasvir had said and that polite cue was the only encouragement her cousin needed to keep talking. She knew she should have hung up; she had plenty to do—but what did most other women her age have to do besides gossip? So she decided to allow her cousin the simple pleasure of acting as commentator and critic on lives that were far more dramatic than her own. Phone to her ear, Jasvir had stood by the window and stared outside, watching the birds perch on the power lines and wondering if they too were looking at her, crowing about the old lady who lived in the giant peach stucco house with the red-tiled roof, the lady who spent her days wandering from room to room. Before she put the house on the market, she'd rented the basement suite to a few international students who were attending a nearby college. Twinkle, her favourite tenant, would often come upstairs to visit and have tea, but now that she had moved out, Jasvir felt utterly alone, falling prey to the distraction that comes with listening to other people's dramas. Since she'd idled on the phone with her cousin, she now felt ill-prepared, underdressed and inferior in ways that only her family could make her feel.

As the doorbell rang a second time, she thought about not answering it. She wished they'd leave the wedding invitations in the mailbox and go on their way, but she knew they wouldn't do that; Darshan was an old-fashioned gloater. She'd deliver them in person even if it meant making a second trip. Jasvir glanced at herself in the foyer mirror. She rarely looked at herself, and when she did she was surprised by the old woman who stared back. She took another hopeless look, adjusted her chunni and opened the door.

"Sat Sri Akal, Phenji," Jasvir said.

Darshan pulled her into a full embrace and then stood back, holding her by both shoulders, staring at her the way a friend might, as if to say, Look at us, here we are, still, after all this time. Yet they weren't friends and hadn't been for decades, not since Jasvir's father had died and left everything to her brother, Seva, Darshan's husband. They stood there for a moment, the awkward familial play-acting reserved for weddings and funerals, until Jasvir ushered them inside with a polite formality.

In the living room, Darshan, her son, Bhajan, and his wife, Raman, sat on the Victorian-style sofa across from Jasvir, their gazes darting artfully at the dated showroom decor, the oversized crystal chandelier, the ornamental brass and glass objects in the curio cabinet—all of it bought when her own children were marrying, when it seemed she had everything, even if only briefly. Aged expectations of another time that now made Jasvir feel embarrassed and irrelevant, as if she too were a relic. Seeming to sense the awkwardness, Bhajan cleared his throat and looked for a moment like he had something real to say, but instead stammered polite inquiries, his stutter cutting him off midsentence. Smiling foolishly, unable to finish his thought, he looked down, folding and wringing his chapped hands in his lap. He had the same dull complexion, bloated belly and wire-thin frame as her father and brother, and she wondered if he too was an alcoholic. Jasvir's son, Navi, who was a doctor, said alcoholism was a disease, a genetic predisposition to addiction that in Jasvir's estimation seemed to inflict only men. She'd never known Indian women to be addicted to anything but suffering,

3

and wondered if that too was a disease. Did sadness pass from mother to daughter at a cellular level? Was she nourished and fortified by guilt? Was hopelessness a genetic imprint? Were her bones fused with shame? If it were true, it would explain so much. She smiled at Darshan who was sitting attentively on the edge of the sofa as if waiting for something to happen.

"So you've come." Jasvir launched into the customary five-minute fiction on how she wished they would visit more often and that they needn't wait for an invitation.

Darshan conceded, as expected. It had been too long. "The farm, it takes so much of our time. You remember how much work it is, and since the expansion it's been so busy."

"The expansion," Jasvir said, repeating the euphemism. She'd heard that they'd borrowed money from questionable sources and were now entangled with unsavoury business partners. "Yes, I've seen the signs." She winced as she recalled the ridiculous Blueberry King billboard with its cartoon crowned berry giving her a thumbs-up every day on her way to visit Dalbir in the hospital. "Very clever."

"It was our Devi's idea. She just finished her business degree," Darshan said.

"You must be so proud of her, and her wedding of course—vadayaan," she said, congratulating Darshan.

"Oh yes, very proud of her. Some children nowadays, they want to be independent. But not our Devi. She is such a good girl. She listens to us, respects our culture."

Jasvir, having registered Darshan's backhanded insult, did not yield in the approval-seeking way she might have when she was younger. "How very nice," she said, wishing she could be more like her cousin, who had a comeback for every criticism. As smart as she was, Jasvir lacked wit. She could not rally in conversation or criticism. It would be hours before she'd think of what she could have said, how she could have let on that everyone knew all about Devi. Devi was just like the other girls, going with boys, wearing revealing clothing, staying out late drinking and doing God knows what else. But in the moment, all she could do was nod and suggest they all have tea.

"No, no. We're fine. Don't go to any trouble," Darshan said, waving her hands on cue as the charade dictated.

Jasvir smiled through her irritation. Perhaps this too was a female affliction, something they were genetically programmed to do, to make nice, make do, make comfort where there was none. "Something cold then?"

"If you insist." Darshan's head see-sawed agreeably. "Water is fine. No ice."

In the kitchen, Jasvir scoured the cupboard looking for some biscuits to put out even though she knew, like everything else, it would only be for show. As she arranged the shortbread, she noted how quiet her guests were being in the other room and the silence made her nervous. It reminded her of all that was unsaid when her father was ill. She'd been his nurse, his cook, his maid. She'd changed his soiled sheets, she'd fed him—and when he no longer remembered anything or anyone, she'd never lost her patience. He died when no one was looking. He died in the middle of the night, yet when she found him he did not look peaceful. He was slack-jawed, his head turned to the side as if someone had wrenched his spirit out of him and tugged him into the next life. Some months later her brother, Seva, had a series of strokes that confined him to his bed. He'd been in a care home ever since. In the years that followed, Jasvir hadn't visited him more than a few times; What do you say to a man who cannot speak? She'd heard the nurses talking to him so she'd tried that, but it seemed cruel to tell him about the weather, her grandchildren, to narrate a world that he could never inhabit. She'd heard that Darshan rarely visited him.

For years now Jasvir had made a point of not driving by the farm, avoiding that stretch of highway altogether—but now with their silly billboards and frequent ads on Punjab Times TV, she was never free of the Dosanjhs. Even their ridiculous jingle, "Blueberry King, Blueberry King, eat like royalty," burrowed into her ear, announcing itself at odd hours of the day. Contrary to the gossip, the estrangement had never been about the money. It was about feeling discarded—and nothing anyone could say would undo that. As she turned the faucet on, she thought of spitting into Darshan's water glass, but of course she did not. She was raised to be respectful, and despite her bitterness, was not prone to acting out. Her anger—no, her frustration—was simmering, a kind of low-grade headache. Just there, at her temples: a dull current buzzing in her brain that she often mistook for tinnitus.

"Here we are." Jasvir set the tray on the coffee table between the two sofas, but as expected, no one took their glass, no one took a sip, no one ate a biscuit, no one said a word—until finally Raman, mother of the bride, spoke.

"Bhuaji, you're moving?" The girl gestured to the realtor's yard sign outside the window. That's how Jasvir saw Raman—still a girl—though she must have been at least fifty by now. Jasvir could still remember the day Raman married her nephew. Fresh-faced, naive and barely twenty; a complete innocent. But that's how it was in those days—girls knew nothing and had nothing— and now here Raman was, her own daughter getting married.

"Oh yes. The house is too big. With your fuferji gone, it only makes sense."

"It must be so hard to live alone," Darshan said, interrupting. "I am so lucky to have had my family with me all of these years." She patted Raman's leg. "Will you go live with Ravi now? I heard you stayed there recently. Or maybe with your son? How is Navi since his divorce?"

"He's fine. His work keeps him busy," Jasvir said, sidestepping any talk about her children that Darshan could spin into gossip.

"And Ravi? I was surprised to hear you were staying there. Is everything alright?"

"She's fine. I was just there helping out with the children when she was at work," Jasvir said, smiling, deflecting.

Darshan nodded, eyeing up Jasvir the way she did when she knew something was being left out. "Kids these days, so busy. Going here and there, working all the time. We always tell our Devi to slow down, but she doesn't listen." Darshan picked up her water and took a tiny sip, grimacing as if it were too cold.

"And how are all the wedding preparations going?" Jasvir asked.

"Never-ending. So many things to do. Devi hired a wedding planner to keep it all straight."

As Darshan continued, talking about their recent no-expense-spared shopping trip for wedding clothes, Jasvir smiled, pretending to care about Chikankari embroidery and the latest fashions. "As long as they are happy, may God keep them."

"So true," Darshan said, making prayer hands. After an awkward silence, she motioned to her son, and commented on the time. "We should be going."

"So soon?" Jasvir said, acting disappointed when all she felt was relief.

"We have so many cards to deliver. We will visit again." Darshan hugged her at the door, then handed Jasvir three envelopes and three boxes of sweets for her to give her family. "Make sure the children come to the wedding. I know they are busy but they must make time."

"Of course." Jasvir stood at the front door, fake smile plastered on, one hand waving and the other clutching her chest.

After they left, Jasvir lay down and practised her breathwork, inhaling for two seconds and exhaling for four until the sharp pain in her chest softened into a dull ache. After having a panic attack in the parking lot of Fruiticana a few months ago that had landed her in the hospital, Jasvir had stayed with her daughter for a few weeks. Ravi, a worrier and fixer by nature, had signed Jasvir up for a yoga class to help her destress and learn how to breathe—as if she had not been breathing just fine for seventy-five years.

Jasvir had felt so foolish that day, and upon entering the locker room had averted her eyes, shielding her vision with a cupped hand as she shuffled by women in all manners of undress. She held her handbag tight across her chest, trying to make herself smaller so as not to bump into anyone. "This is for young people," she'd told Ravi, who had crouched down beside her to help her take her sneakers off the very same way Jasvir had done when Ravi was in kindergarten. Inside the studio, women who looked like slightly altered versions of each other in their matching bras and tight pants rolled out their mats in perfect rows in front of Karma, the instructor, who was elevated on a small stage. Karma wore a headset microphone, and while standing in mountain pose told them, "Feel your breath, and ground yourself." While the others followed along with eyes closed, Jasvir kept hers open and glanced around the room of sweaty women. Mountain pose, child's pose, downward dog, warrior—these rows of women, including

Ravi, moved as if they were one person. Jasvir floundered in the dry heat, and wrapped her chunni around her head to keep the sweat out of her eyes. Always a movement or two behind, she felt like her body was a twig ready to snap. She did not understand how these women, her daughter included, could fold themselves in such ways. Her kameez clung to her torso and, as she stood there in a pool of her own sweat, she could have sworn she heard someone snicker. She turned to see two young blonde women, both with nose rings, staring at her. Ravi insisted they weren't staring at her because she was Indian, but because she wore her salwar kameez to a hot yoga class instead of wearing the clothes that Ravi had bought for her. Jasvir had scoffed that it made no difference. "These yoga people in their hundred-dollar la-lu-lu-la pants are just like the goras who like butter chicken and drink masala chai; they want the Indianness without the Indians. Just like that Karma and her namaste," Jasvir said, mocking the way Karma had anglicized the word, the way she bowed with folded hands at the end of class. Jasvir knew that her daughter, who called to check on her every day, was just trying to help, but what she wanted most was to not be worried about like a burdensome adult-child. What she wanted was to be left alone, to be the person that could just *be*. Had she ever just been? Can any woman just be, or does every woman always have to be something to someone else? She wanted to quiet that thought, to snuff it out; no good had ever come from it.

Seeing Darshan had upset her in ways she hadn't expected; she thought she was finished with the past and yet there it was, lurking in her own body, an exhaustion that lulled her to sleep. When Jasvir woke up from her nap, she was surprised that the sun was still up. Time was slow like that, unfair in its keeping since Dalbir had died. She'd sped through the best parts of life, and now all she had were regrets and memories to keep her company. Although she'd grown up in India and settled in Canada, she had seen nothing of the world. When she went to stay with Ravi in Vancouver—only thirty minutes from home—it felt foreign to her, and this filled her with a great and surprising sadness. She had never been anywhere. All of her trips to India were simply home to airport to home with no stops in between. Why she had never paused to see the world around her, she couldn't say—she'd never asked, and now who was there to ask? Sometimes she wondered what her life might have been if she'd thought to ask. Although she never went to college, she had a way with numbers, easily solving the complex equations her brother, Seva, was working on. She couldn't explain how she did it—numbers just made sense to her, a perfect and complete language. Had she been a boy, she would have been someone. An engineer, a doctor, a scientist—she could have been something! When Navi was in medical school she'd leafed through his textbooks, and when he wasn't home she would sit at his desk, put on her glasses and pore over the books as if she could somehow will herself to understand the complex anatomy the way she understood math. Most people assumed Navi had inherited his mind from his father, and when they said so, she didn't correct them.

Dalbir had been a stoic man and his partiality for routines had made life go by in a predictable, well-paced way. Because he was quiet, some mistook him for passive, but, in fact, beneath his silence was a definitive way of being, an obstinate nature, a forcefulness which left no room for interpretation. He wasn't abusive the way other men of his generation sometimes were, and had raised his hand only once. Even now she couldn't remember why, only that he had, and that he'd done so in front of the children—and how she'd felt his humiliation as if it was her own. Women feel a type of shame that is never their own. This is one thing she knew for certain. Despite this, she did miss him; marriage was the habituation of two people and now she was just adrift with no habits of her own. Can you teach an old dog new tricks? She'd heard this expression on TV once and finally understood what it meant. She sat up and looked around the room at all that would need to be sorted and packed, a lifetime of things. It was enough to make her chest tighten up, and she wondered if Ravi was right to disapprove of her selling the house and moving to False Creek.

It was while staying with Ravi that Jasvir had stumbled upon the showroom during one of her morning walks. Inside, she'd watched the way others moved about the unit, talking about the finishes and crown moulding, inquiring about the amenities and strata fees as they helped themselves to the complimentary coffee and oatmeal cookies. She mimicked the other prospective buyers and opened closets and cupboards, tried the light switches and remarked on the radiant floor heating. In the bedroom, she sat on the king-sized bed, staring out the window at the boats that dotted the calm waters, and felt a deep sense of peace. She took from her handbag the prepaid phone that Ravi had bought her for emergencies and called her daughter. The realtor, concerned about Jasvir overstaying her welcome, hovered, asking if she had any questions every few minutes, and was visibly relieved when a confused Ravi finally came to collect her. "Are you serious? Why move now?" she'd asked. Jasvir, who was still staring out the window at the gleaming city, the sea and mountains, the gradient shades of blue, was serious. But how could she explain to her daughter that for the first time in her life, she was looking out at the world with no one to deny her. Even she found it hard to believe.

Now, with only a few weeks to closing date, she felt herself falling into old patterns of doubt and confinement. Life was easier when it was predictable. She got up from the couch to make some ginger tea. No longer bothering to go to the effort of crushing cardamom and fennel, she simply put the kettle on and waited for the whistle before dropping a tea bag into a mug. Between bitter sips, she picked up the wedding invitation. Unable to make out the lettering, she slipped on the reading glasses she wore on a chain around her neck and held the card at arm's length, tilting her head up and down until the letters came into focus. The ornate card had fuchsia paisleys and elephants adorning each corner, and when she opened it, gilt confetti fell ceremoniously into her lap. The invitation, with its many event inserts, detailed the full week of functions from the sangeet party to the wedding reception. She ran her fingers over the embossed lettering, the glitter on her hands reminding her of craft time with Ravi's daughter. She thought about what her cousin had told her about the groom's plans to arrive at the wedding on an elephant. "A circus!" That's what Ravi would say about the entire production. Jasvir picked up the phone and called her daughter.

"Darshan Mamiji came over," she said, getting right to it. "Remember, I told you her granddaughter is getting married in six weeks."

"Right, yeah, to the sweet shop family, right? Hey, put that down!" Ravi said, hollering to her daughter in the background. "Sorry Mom."

"It's okay," Jasvir said; she used to have the same habit of talking to two people at once. "She dropped off cards and ladoos for you and your brother."

"Oh yeah?"

"Yeah," she said, mocking her daughter's casual English.

"Are they from Baby Nanak's?"

"No, they're from A-1 Sweets," she said, running her hands over the embossed initials on the box.

"Going with the competition. Kind of insulting, no?"

"Yes, that's exactly the point," Jasvir said, explaining how she'd heard that the families were embroiled in petty disputes. "You know your Darshan mamiji, she thinks she's better than everyone. She wanted her granddaughter to marry someone richer, and the boy's family wanted him to marry a doctor, so neither of them are happy about this love marriage." Jasvir could tell her daughter was preoccupied, busy mothering in the background, only half listening, only half existing. "I thought I'd come by, drop the cards and ladoos off for you."

"Thanks, but no. You know I shouldn't be eating that junk."

"Well maybe Navi will eat them. I can go there first."

"No Mom, he won't. He's on keto."

"Kato?"

"No, keto. It's his new diet."

"Kato, keto, what's the difference?" she said, remembering now that he'd forsaken all sugar. She'd thought it a joyless way to live, and when she'd told him as much they'd had a small argument about her never being supportive, and when she said that she didn't want to fight he said that he wasn't fighting, he was just talking, and this had made her go quiet just as she had always done with his father. "Well I could still bring you yours, for the kids."

"No, it's okay, really."

"But they love sweets."

"So did I when I was a kid but you never let us have any."

"What's that supposed to mean?"

"You were strict is all I'm saying." She paused. "I just wish you'd been more like you are now."

Jasvir nodded. "Times were different. I did my best."

"I know you did. I'm just saying, it would have been nice."

"Lots of things would have been nice," she said, avoiding the regret that had darkened every corner of her life these last months. She'd done her best, worked two jobs, taken care of everyone—What more could she have done? And here her daughter was a grown woman—a mother no less—asking her for what, an apology? She wondered what there was to say. As a girl, had her daughter really never seen how tired she was from washing dishes all day in a hotel restaurant where she couldn't afford to eat? And, as a woman, had Ravi really never noticed the smallness of her mother's life and how all Jasvir wanted for her children was more than she'd had for herself? No, her daughter had never seen any of this, and trying to explain it to her now was not worth the effort. "What do you want me to do about the ladoos?" she asked, growing agitated looking at the boxes.

"Give them to a neighbour or something. Just don't you eat them, Mom. You have to watch your sugar levels."

Jasvir wished Twinkle still lived in the basement; she would have eaten the ladoos. They would have enjoyed them together and gossiped about the wedding, and Twinkle—who worked at Goldie's Palace and saw all the season's parties—would have told her the latest gupshup about who was doing what and where. "What about the card? Will you at least come to the wedding or do I have to throw that out too?"

"I have to check my schedule. Maybe Navi can go with you this time."

"You should both come. It won't look good if you aren't there. We're family. Tell me, when I'm dead will you never see any of my relatives again?" she asked, guilting her daughter.

"Oh come on, Mom, even you hate them."

"I don't hate them," she lied. "Besides, they're your cousins. You must go."

"No, they aren't my cousins. It's my cousin's kid, who I wouldn't recognize in a grocery store if I met her. Why these people need to keep having these big fat Indian weddings is beyond me."

"*These* people? These people are your people. Your family."

"Okay, sorry. I wasn't trying to argue with you."

"We're not fighting, we're just talking." Jasvir's tone softened. "Are you sure you don't want me to come by with the ladoos?" she asked.

"Positive," Ravi said. "But I was thinking that I could come by on the weekend and help with the packing."

"That would be nice." Jasvir looked around at the empty boxes. She was excited about the condo, about starting a new life, but now that she could do what she wanted, she didn't know where to begin. How do you start over, and what do you leave behind? "You know, I don't know what I'm supposed to do with all of it—Navi's textbooks, your father's things. Shall I get rid of them too? Shall I throw everything away?" Jasvir could hear herself start to spiral, could feel the panic creeping up her throat. Her children had assumed her panic attacks were about their father's death, and though of course she did miss Dalbir, her grief was not so much for him as it was for herself. Now alone, she saw all that she'd lost, every moment, every possibility—all the things she'd done and not done pressing on her chest until she couldn't breathe.

"Mom, relax, we'll do it together."

"I am relaxed. In fact, I am doing my yoga breathing right now," she said, exaggerating her breath. "Namaste." She set the receiver down and opened one of the gold boxes, admiring the ladoos lined up like nine little suns in rows of three by three. She took one out and held it in the air before biting into it like an apple. She closed her eyes as the pebbled exterior crumbled into her mouth. Oh such sweetness! What a shame to throw them away, she thought, eating another and then another, exhausting her taste buds with a thickening sameness.

DEAR AUNTIE

THE WEDDING EDITION WAS *AWAAZ*'S MOST PROFITABLE ISSUE AND earned enough advertising revenue to keep the local magazine afloat all year long. At only 250 pages it wasn't anywhere close to the iconic September issue of *Vogue* that first inspired Priya's love of fashion, nor did it have any of the journalistic depth she appreciated in the *Atlantic*, or the *New York Times*, but it was their most popular issue—and by *popular*, she meant least pulped. *Awaaz* was a free monthly magazine that focused on the local Punjabi community and whose margins were devoted to promoting small businesses like Fancy Fashions, Goldie's Palace, Baby Nanak's Sweet Shop and countless others. When Priya finished her journalism degree she hadn't expected that she'd be a freelance writer and regular contributor to *Awaaz*, "the Voice of Our Community." She'd watched her peers find placements with local TV stations, radio broadcasters and newspapers, while almost all of her applications went unanswered. According to one producer, she didn't have the face for TV. She took that to mean that she was too dark, and that her face didn't conform to the coveted golden ratio. Even her mother had noticed that the news hour's Punjabi anchorwoman's nose had become slimmer and her complexion brightened. "Jas looks different, Jas looks so good, Jas lost weight," she'd say, calling her by name as if she knew her. At dinner one night, she'd suggested that Priya try the same lightening creams and contouring makeup, and they'd argued about that and about all the other ways Priya felt her mother had tried to modify and manipulate her into being a better version of herself. After being turned down by the local TV stations Priya had tried radio but was told her voice was too sharp, the uptalk signalling her age. Regardless of how many voice lessons she took, she could not find her inner baritone the way Oprah had. She'd attempted to get an internship at one of the daily national papers but didn't know the right people—or the white people, as her father said—to get her foot in the door. After six months of unemployment, her father's uncle, Dalbir, mentioned he had a friend who owned a magazine and would put in a word. At the time she thought it would be her starter job, but she'd been working there and selling freelance clickbait articles to the highest bidder ever since. She told herself it wasn't so bad, at least she got to work in her pajamas most of the day, but then whenever she read *The Globe and Mail* and recognized the name of a classmate in a byline she felt that old familiar mix- ture of envy and self-loathing bubble up. It was that same feeling that had driven her to straighten her frizzy curls, to get laser hair removal, to get straight *A*s in school, to edit the school paper, yet none of it had helped. No ceilings had been broken. She was still just the brown girl who wanted to be a journalist.

When she first started at *Awaaz* she'd cornered Teja—her middle-aged, pot-bellied editor who always wore short-sleeved button-ups—and pitched hard-hitting story ideas that she'd scribbled in her notebook throughout the week.

"Surrey gangland slayings," she'd suggested hopefully.

"No."

"But there have been three shootings this month alone."

"No."

"Domestic violence?"

"No," he'd said, looking up at her over the top of his glasses.

"What, why? It's an epidemic in our community."

"It's an epidemic in every community. Ours is no different."

"Precisely."

"Still no."

"The politics of food. Farming Punjab's breadbasket."

"No."

"Come on, really? We're the only ones not covering the farming protests. My uncle was there earlier this year and he told me about the stats on farmer suicides. We could write about that: No living, no life," she said. "Now that's a story."

"No. We aren't a political magazine, Priya, and we don't do social commentary either. What we do here is elevate our community. We showcase our success stories."

"Some would call that propaganda."

"It's only propaganda if it's not true. I don't see why the news should only report on our failings or our struggles."

She nodded, indicating that she understood. It was his magazine, his vision, so she went along with his agenda—and this year he'd finally let her pen some cover stories. She'd interviewed a hockey player who could go pro ("He Shoots, He Scores") and an academic who was championing South Asian studies in k–12 ("Our History, Our Pride"). In addition to writing feature stories, she wrote the Dear Auntie column, where readers wrote in asking for advice to their everyday problems—so long as those problems reflected the magazine's conservative values. She answered letters about how to improve one's GPA, how to fit in with the in-laws and how to balance work and family, but the *Dear Auntie, I'm pregnant and don't want the baby. What should I do?* and *Dear Auntie, I think I'm gay* letters were never published. It was those submissions that inspired her to create an online alternate Dear Auntie persona. Within months she'd gone viral, but because she used filters on her face and put on the Bollywood accent she'd perfected after having grown up on a steady diet of Indian dramas, no one knew her real identity. What had started as an act of altruism to deliver much-needed advice had morphed into influencing. Affiliate cash for clicks made up for the shortfall in her personal finances, and soon she was posting bridal buys along with her relationship and life tips in breezy twenty-second video clips. Even though she wasn't married, her work on the wedding issue of *Awaaz* made her feel like less of a fraud.

"Inspiration for your own wedding!" her colleagues said whenever they'd ask her to write bridal style sections or columns about current trends. But even writing formulaic articles about the season's muted pastels, floral silks and destination wedding tips was better than writing the matrimonial section.

"Come on, everyone loves a good love story, Priya!" Teja said, when in her first year at the magazine she moaned at having to interview the newly married or about-to-be-married couples about their weddings, proposal stories, best relationship advice and future plans. He was right though, everyone loved love. All year long readers would send in their love stories hoping to be selected for the feature spread that chronicled a couple's entire wedding. She understood the allure; everyone wanted to be that girl who fell in love and lived happily ever after. Like so many women, Priya indulged in rom-coms and could appreciate a good meet-cute or love-is-all-you-need epiphany. She was especially fond of the ones where a high-powered career woman returns home for Christmas and falls back in love with her never-left-home first boyfriend who wears plaid flannel shirts. She liked the idea that love could be as simple as returning to one's past, even though for her it had never been true. She hadn't had a relationship in three years, hadn't had a real date in months and was the only person in her friend group who was still single. The previous year she'd been a bridesmaid three times and gone to seven weddings. Despite everyone's efforts to be original, her memories of them were interchangeable, the same way her columns about the matrimonial couples were: all the same variation of happy, lucky and in love. They were everything she wasn't; she felt sorry for them and resented them all at once.

This wedding season the feature couple's headline was "A Berry Sweet Couple: Blueberry Queen Devinder Dosanjh Weds Baby Nanak's Sweet Shop Namesake Nanak Atwal." Though her great-uncle had been related to the Dosanjh family through marriage, she'd never met Devi and didn't know anything about Nanak, except that her first cousin used to date his older brother. Everyone thought they'd get married and had it not been for his accident they probably would have. She remembered her cousin saying, "I didn't sign up for this," as a justification for dumping him just a few weeks after he was home from the hospital. No one knew what to say to that, but Priya thought about it a lot, especially as she worked on the matrimonials. People had put love on a checklist; it was a task, something to execute. Date for a year, meet the parents, get engaged, plan a lavish wedding, travel to an

Instagram-worthy honeymoon spot, build a house, get pregnant, have a baby shower, throw baby's first birthday party in a banquet hall, have another baby, post family pictures in matching seasonal outfits, document parties and events on socials and live happily ever after. A list was not a life. She wished she could tell the couples she interviewed that, but even if she did, they would never listen to her, because what could a thirty-year-old single Indian girl know about love? No one wanted to know the truth about love. Even her Dear Auntie followers hit back if her posts weren't funny or entertaining enough. The things she did to keep their attention. Her last post was titled "Wedding Glow-Ups and Blow-Ups: A Montage of Makeovers and Bridesmaid Cat Fights." It had more hearts than any other post, which was simultaneously disheartening. She wondered where all the smart people had gone, and the more Dear Auntie followers she got, the more she was convinced that her generation's veneer had become their identity; they were all Insta people. She suspected Devinder and Nanak would be the same.

She met them at a local coffee shop on a Sunday afternoon. He ordered an Americano and she ordered a non-fat chai tea latte with extra foam, laughing about the terrible translation in ordering "tea tea" the way every Indian person did. She was pretty in the way girls with money are: great dental work, highlighted hair, regular facials and perfectly arched brows—threaded or maybe microbladed. He was a regular-looking guy with manscaped stubble and a perfect jaw. He had the same fade as his friends, was wearing Adidas track pants and a hoodie. He had not yet been fully made over in the way she'd noticed the newlywed husbands were; they showed up looking expensive, coordinated and accessorized with some subtle Gucci stripe.

"Thanks again for meeting me," Priya said as she put her phone on the table between them. "Do you mind if I record this? It's just easier than taking notes."

"Yeah, of course. No worries." Devinder had a nasal pitch, not congested but pinched, and when she spoke, she punctuated syllables, slicing up words. Everything about her was sharp and constructed, from her elevated athleisure attire to her small gold hoop earrings. She was on trend, on point, and from what Priya had gathered from a Dear Auntie message she'd received from an @DeeDee last night, she might have also been on edge. *Dear Auntie, I'm getting married soon but have feelings for someone else. What should I do?* @DeeDee was a new account with no followers, and had a stock image as a profile picture; it could have been anyone, but the idea that it could be Devinder Dosanjh had sparked Priya's curiosity. As she made small talk, she looked for clues, signs of discontent, something to make this interview more interesting.

"So, let's start with an easy one. Devinder, Nanak, tell me, how did you meet?"

"Please, call us Devi and Baby—everyone does," Devi said.

"Okay. So, how did you meet?"

They looked at each other, gauging who would answer, who would take the lead. "At school, UBC," Devi said.

"Same class?"

"No, at a party—not a frat party or anything like that. Just a social thing. A few friends and friends of friends, of course. Nothing crazy. He was actually there with someone else at the time, but even so, I felt a connection. I knew right away that he was the one."

"Oh, so he had a girlfriend at the time?"

"Well, I wouldn't say that." Devi said, biting her lip. "Anne was just a friend . . . They worked together . . . Are you going to write that in the article?" she asked, leaning in.

"No, of course not. Just getting background details. And how about you? Is he your first love?"

"Well, um. Yes, of course he is."

Priya could tell Devi was nervous. She smiled at the end of every sentence the way a child would when looking for approval. "What was it about him?"

Devi looked up and twirled the end of her hair. "I guess he seemed different from all the other guys his age. He was quiet and nice," she said, glancing at Baby, who was texting. She smiled and grabbed his hand. "Could you not right now?"

"Sorry," he said, putting his phone away.

"It's just wedding stuff," she said to Priya, who had noticed the frustration in her tone. "So many details. Our phones are going off non-stop."

"I understand," she said, only half listening as Devi talked about the thousand-plus guest list, the DJ flying in from Mumbai and all the assorted details that had consumed the better part of the last year.

"So, how long have you known each other?" Priya directed her question at Baby.

"It's been, what, four years now, right?" Baby said, putting his arm around Devi.

"Almost five," she said, correcting him. "He's so bad with dates."

"I am not."

"You are so." She giggled and nudged him. "You almost forgot our anniversary last month!"

"Yeah, the anniversary of the day we met. Who remembers that?" he said, laughing.

"I do," Devi said, her smile tight. "First meeting, first date, first kiss. I remember all of it." Devi sat up straighter and pivoted away from him in her seat. It was a small movement, a gesture that most people wouldn't have noticed, but Priya recognized the discontent. It had been that way for her in her past relationship, small disputes and layered land mines.

"So, Baby, tell me: What was it that attracted you to Devi?"

"I don't know." He shrugged. "Probably her confidence. She likes to be the centre of attention, doesn't take no for an answer. You can't really help but notice her."

"You say it like it's a bad thing," Devi said.

"I didn't mean it like that. I meant that you're a go-getter."

"Sure," she said, forcing a smile.

Having interviewed so many couples, Priya could easily sense the hostility between them. Whether it was the stress of the wedding or an unresolved argument, the tension was just under the surface, the relationship buckling at fault lines. It was just enough to make anyone second-guess their feelings the same way @Deedee was.

If Priya listened carefully, she could almost hear the horsemen of marriage apocalypse galloping toward Devi and Baby. She'd written about those horsemen in a psychology paper in her first year of university, and had since seen them everywhere. Gottman's four signs of relational dysfunction: criticism, contempt, defensiveness and stonewalling. They all seemed so commonplace, it was a wonder that any relationship lasted. Hers certainly hadn't, and in that she wasn't alone; most of the couples she interviewed would get divorced or disenchanted within a few years. She wanted to warn them, to give them some Dear Auntie advice, to tell them that they were already on the verge of hating all the things they loved about each other. If Devi was this @Deedee that had written in about her pre-wedding feelings for someone else, she was probably having feelings for someone that was more like her. Opposites may attract, but ultimately, everyone wants a partner that's just like them; people mistake sameness for understanding. As she thought about the Dear Auntie letter, she began asking more pointed questions. What do you love about each other? What are your pet peeves about each other? What are you most looking forward to about your wedding? What's next for the both of you? Do you want a family?

Mostly it was Devi responding with canned answers; like so many girls, she'd been rehearsing for this her whole life. Priya had been in love once. Once was enough. He cheated on her with a trusted friend and then married said friend. She lost them both; it broke her. Someone should write about that—someone should Dear Auntie that shit.

"Just a few more questions," she said, already anticipating their answers. "What advice do you have for other couples?"

"I don't know, everyone's so different," Devi said.

"Maybe that's it, you know," Baby added. "You have to know each other, know how you're different and the same, and respect that. Don't try to change each other. Meet each other where you're at. Does that make sense?"

"Aw, Baby," Devi said, reaching for his hand. "I love you. See why I love him?" she said, her eyes soft and wide, doe-like and hopeful.

"That's great, really great advice." Priya, aware of how locked into each other they suddenly were, shifted awkwardly in her seat. "Well, I think I have what I need," she said, ending the interview prematurely. "I'll connect with your photographer about a few photos for the feature. You're using Rish, right?"

Devi nodded. "You know him?"

"Yeah, he does freelance work for the magazine."

"He's so talented, right?"

"He is." Priya could tell Devi was digging, looking for a morsel, some tidbit that she could save or trade, but for what, she wasn't sure.

"And single I hear," Devi said, eyebrows up.

"Yeah, I guess." Priya wondered if Devi knew that she'd hooked up with Rish at a party a few months ago; people were always talking. "I should get going."

"Wait," Devi said, taking an invitation out of her purse. "We'd love it if you came. No better way to write our wedding story than to be there with us on the big day."

"Thank you. That's very thoughtful," she said as she collected her things. "I'll be in touch."

From her parked car, Priya watched Devi and Baby leave hand in hand a few minutes later. She observed the way they walked, a playful weaving in and away from each other as they strolled down the street. Curious, Priya felt that part of her wanted to follow them, to see where they went, if they stopped to buy fresh flowers at the corner market, if they ducked into a matinee, if they walked together endlessly, arms slung loosely around shoulders and hips, if they were really in love.

As Priya started her car, she reflected on the interview. She didn't know why she was in such a hurry to leave, only that she was, that they'd surprised her. Those horsemen that she'd thought she'd heard were always just racing around in her head. Galloping and galloping.

BASIC BABY

BABY WAS SITTING IN HIS PARKED CAR IN FRONT OF THE OLD SWEET shop building for the second time this week. He hadn't set out to go there, and yet there he was, car still on, windshield wipers swiping every few seconds, defroster blasting, fog circles clearing. His family hadn't lived in the apartment above the shop for over ten years, yet in his mind it was home, and when he wasn't thinking about where he was going or what he was doing, he ended up navigating the familiar childhood streets of there and back again—sometimes until he'd gone too far and had to aggressively cross three lanes of traffic or U-turn to course correct. He'd been sixteen when they moved into the house with the gated driveway and three garages, a house where he and his older brother, Gobind, no longer had to share a bedroom or even a bathroom, for the house had many. "Six toilets!" He can still remember how excited his mother was about this even though she'd often complained about having to clean the one bathroom they'd all shared in the apartment. But the not sharing—to his mother—was a good thing. "Walk-in closets, a butler's pantry, ensuites, two family rooms and a living room," she'd said when they toured the house. "Think of all the space you'll have!"

When they moved in, Baby had been unable to sleep. He'd grown used to the sound of sirens, the sounds of the homeless scavenging for scraps in the dumpster out back, and now all he heard was the occasional car slowing down on the nearby traffic-calming roundabout. On the weekends, sometimes hours would pass by without him seeing anyone; he actually had to look for his mother, his brother, his father, when previously they'd always been right in front of him, always there in his way, in his space, encroaching, questioning, interfering—and to his surprise it was that proximity that he missed the most, the being next to, the being with, the never being alone that he suddenly longed for.

A buzzing: his phone in the cup holder lit up. It was Devi. He didn't answer. He couldn't listen the way she wanted him to, and each time she noticed that he was only *yeah*-ing her, that he didn't really care about the caterer, the photographer or the wedding planner, she freaked out. She'd become one of those women on reality shows, one of those women who point their fingers or palms at someone's face to say no, as if the word were not enough. He tucked the phone into his pocket and turned off the engine, watching as the rain fell onto the windshield, blurring the blinking neon Open sign in front of him.

The door chimed, announcing his arrival.

"About time you came in." Hassan, dressed in his usual silk shirt and dress slacks, was standing behind the front counter cracking rolls of quarters into the cash register. "You've been sitting in your car for thirty minutes." Hassan tried to stifle his grin but Baby knew he was happy to see him.

"So what, you're stalking me now?" Baby slid into his favourite booth, the one that was closest to the counter and gave the best view of the TV, the same one he and Gobind sat at every day after school when his parents were working and they were still too little to stay upstairs by themselves. He stared up at the screen, the hockey game on but muted.

"I should say the same. Eleven years and I haven't been able to get rid of you," Hassan said, still smiling. "Hungry?" He didn't wait for Baby to answer and yelled to the cook, "Kebab and fries for Baby."

Everyone called Nanak Baby on account of the sweet shop. Most people assumed the family business was named after him, or that he was named after the business, but neither was true. His parents had meant to call the shop Baba Nanak's just like the one his baba had in India, but a print error at the sign shop had changed that. His father had blamed his mother for not filling in the form properly—her handwriting was crowded, she should have printed it in capital letters like the instructions said—and his mother had blamed his father for not checking the proof properly. But fault did nothing to solve the matter, and since they couldn't afford a new awning and sign, the name was changed and his infant likeness was added to the sweet box. Aunties—even the ones who didn't know him—still pinched his cheeks and remarked on what a cute baby he was as if he were still the fat little baby on the box. As much as he hated being called Baby, it was better than being called Ladoo, or Gulab Jamun, or all the other pet names his Boston Auntie had for him.

Baby turned up the volume on the TV. He wasn't a big hockey fan but the sound of the game was comforting—the commentator's flat voice calling out plays and passes, the hushed anticipation as a player broke away down the ice, the crowd erupting—all of it reminded him of growing up here, above the shop. He and Gobind used to play hockey by the dumpster in the alley behind the shop, but with just the two of them it wasn't much of a game. Occasionally, when his father had time, he would come out and play—but with only two sticks it was mostly just slapshot practice. His father in his dirty white apron and second-hand Fair Isle sweater, his father with his thick moustache and full head of hair, his father who smelled like Old Spice and frying oil, yelling out "He shoots, he scores!" before dropping his stick and taking a victory lap around the metal bin.

If Baby remembered hard enough, he could picture the sweet shop just as it was before Hassan had leased it. Where the counter was now used to be where the glass display case of ladoos, barfis, jalebis and gulab jamuns had been, and just adjacent to that there had been a beaded curtain covering the doorway into the kitchen. The walls were the same drab beige, the burgundy vinyl bench seating and easy-clean Formica tabletops were the same; almost everything was the same except the smells. His bibi, who back then had sat in the corner watching her Indian dramas on TV, would say that the change in cuisine meant something—if she were still alive. The heavenly smell of sweets—nectar, spun sugar, golden frying oil—or the smell of charred meat, muscle fat and bone broiled and barbecued on a stick—"Which do you prefer?" Like a mystic, she made the simple profound, every word a world of meaning just out of Baby's reach. She'd died a few years before Gobind's accident, and in that Baby found meaning; if she'd lived she would have lost faith the way the rest of them had. No one was the same after the accident. Every happiness, including Baby's upcoming wedding, was tinged with the sadness of knowing that Gobind would never have the life he deserved.

"You want a soda?" Hassan asked, plating the food on a plastic tray.

"Sure." Baby got up to pour one from the fountain machine.

"No, no, get a bottle from the fridge," Hassan said. "On the house."

"You sure?" Baby knew that Hassan diluted the soda mixture to save money, and that money was always tight. He'd heard his parents complaining about the occasional bounced rent cheque.

"Only the best for you," he said, sitting across from Baby in the booth. "So tell me, how are things? How is your family?"

"Good I guess."

"You guess? You don't know? Kids. You know nothing these days." He pushed the tray closer to Baby. "Eat, eat."

Baby doused his fries in hot sauce, aware that Hassan was watching him eat the way he always did. When they'd met, Hassan said Baby reminded him of his younger brother. It had been years since Hassan had seen or heard from him. Sometimes when Baby looked at Hassan he could see how lonely he was. Hassan didn't know if his brother was alive or dead, if he was somewhere or nowhere, maybe in a refugee camp, maybe drowned—Who could say? Baby assumed Hassan was Syrian, but he couldn't quite place the accent and he'd never asked; now it was too late to ask the questions he should have asked long ago. Now the query would be a knife, a needle, an exhumation. Some things are better left in the ground. That's what Baby's bibi would have said about it.

"Want some?" he asked, aware that Hassan was still watching him eat.

"No, no. Doctor says I have to watch my cholesterol." He smiled at Baby's food face, that funny back-and-forth way he shook his head and closed his eyes when he was chewing.

"Is okay?" Hassan asked, fishing for compliments.

Face stuffed, Baby nodded. "So good."

"The best." Hassan pointed to the small plaque on the wall. He'd been presented with the award for best Middle Eastern restaurant last year by the local paper. He'd photocopied the article and included a copy with every takeout order. Baby Nanak's Sweet Shop had also been named the best in its category every year since they'd opened; Baby's parents had reinvested all their profits into the new shops, and now, into a line of frozen desserts to be sold in a national grocery chain. As exciting as this was, they were, as his mother said, cash-poor. With the wedding bills mounting on top of Gobind's medical expenses, his father was driving a taxi to make ends meet.

When Baby got up in the morning his father was often just getting home, and they'd sit together drinking chai, not saying anything. His father's face was thin and ashy, and sometimes Baby thought that if he spoke too loud he might disintegrate and fall away from himself just like the dandelions he and Gobind used to make wishes on. Like them, his father was spent.

"So how are things?" Hassan asked.

"You know, busy—the wedding and all. Speaking of which, did you get the card? You're coming, right?"

"Of course, wouldn't miss it. Your parents must be very excited."

"Yeah, sure. I guess."

Hassan made a face. "You guess or you're sure?"

"It's stressful, that's all. The closer it gets the more freaked out they get about all the details, the out-of-town relatives, the food, the decorations—it's all just happening, you know? Not to me, just around me—but it's supposed to be *my* wedding."

Hassan slapped the table with one hand. "Ha!" He shook his head as if Baby had missed the obvious. "Your wedding isn't *your* wedding. It's your families' wedding. Two families," he said, demonstrating by clasping his hands together, "become one. This wedding is more important to them than it is to you."

"Now you sound like my mom."

"She's a sensible woman. You should listen to her. So smart."

"Yeah, I suppose," he said, thinking about her plans for the business. Baby Nanak's might have been his father's family business, but it was his mother who had made the expansion possible.

"And how about your brother—how is he these days?"

"He's okay, I guess."

"Again with the guessing," Hassan said, shaking his head. "I bet it's hard for him to see you getting married. He's the older brother after all."

"Nah, he's not like that."

"Maybe not, but I'm sure watching you getting married, finishing school, it reminds him of what he doesn't have."

"Just because he's in a chair doesn't mean he can't have a good life."

"Easy for you to say. Imagine how it is for him."

"I don't have to imagine," Baby said, trying not to sound defensive. Ever since the accident, all he wanted to do was to make sure everyone was okay because it was so obvious no one was. Baby had already taken on all that had been expected of Gobind, but it never seemed to be enough for anyone. "I see him every day. He's my brother."

"Exactly. He's your brother. She's your mother. He's your father. And this wedding is about them as much as it is about you. My wedding day was the happiest day of my life, not just because I was getting married, but because my whole family was with me." Hassan went quiet and Baby recognized the glow of nostalgia, the glint in the eye, remnants of some ordinary joy. "Don't take that for granted."

"You've got a point."

Hassan eyed his empty plate. "You want seconds?"

"Nah, I'm stuffed. I should get going."

"Let me pack something for your brother. Next time, bring him with you."

"Sure." Baby got up to pay, but Hassan refused.

While he waited for Hassan to bag the Styrofoam contain-ers, Baby checked his phone. He had three more missed calls from Devi and finally called her back.

"Where have you been?" she asked.

"Nowhere—I mean, busy. You know."

"Well, I've been calling."

"I know. This is me calling you back. What's up?"

"I got the rough cut of the video. Are you coming over tonight?"

He grabbed the plastic bags from Hassan and mouthed Thank you. "I hadn't planned on it."

"Well, can you?" Her voice was a serrated ultimatum.

Hands full, he pushed the door open with his shoulder. It was still raining outside and he stood under the awning watch-ing the rain drip off the canopy. "I don't know. I just picked up takeout from Hassan's for Gobi."

"Ugh, I don't know why you like that place so much. Hassan gives me the creeps, so sleazy in his satin shirts and gold chain."

Baby went quiet, never knowing quite what to say when she punched down like that.

"So, are you coming or not?"

"No, not tonight. I can't."

"What about the video?"

"Just send me the link and I'll watch it."

"Fine." She said it like a complete sentence and hung up.

WHEN BABY GOT HOME, HE SNUCK IN THROUGH THE SIDE DOOR TO avoid his father, who was supervising the workers measuring the yard for the party tents. Although their house was large enough to host the pre-wedding events, his mother didn't want people walking inside and ruining her carpet, so she had rented party tents and even a row of porta-potties. To appease the neighbours, who otherwise might complain about the comings and goings of guests, the street parking and loud parties, his mother had invited them all to the wedding. Every time Baby saw Mrs. Haskill from down the street she'd say, "Sat Sri Akal," and tell him how excited she was. "I've never been to an East Indian wedding." And then she'd go on to tell him something about an Indian co-worker she'd once had, like that mattered, like he should know the guy.

Baby took off his coat and hung it to dry before joining his brother in the family room. "What are you doing?"

"Running for public office. What does it look like I'm doing?" Gobind adjusted his gaming headset. "Fuck no, shoot!" he yelled.

Baby held up the brown bag. "From the kebab shop. Hassan says hi."

"Hi back. Bring it over."

Baby unpacked the bag in front of Gobind, who swatted at his brother to get out of the way. "I'm in a game."

Baby flopped down on the couch next to him. With all the hours that Gobind had spent gaming these last years he could easily have gone pro but he couldn't be bothered, which was the same thing he said about going to back to school to finish his degree. Of the brothers, Gobind was the smarter one, the one who everyone liked, the one who made friends easily. When

36

they'd moved and switched high schools Gobind hadn't struggled to make friends the way Baby had, and had even let Baby hang out with him until he made his own friends. Baby had heard about the Surrey Jacks; some of their affiliations weren't so great, but Gobind told him he had it under control. "Just chill bro. I've got this," he'd said. Baby should have pressed him on it; he should have been direct and asked him where he got so much cash and why he had a burner. But part of him didn't want to know—it was easier that way.

He was supposed to have gone to the club with Gobind the night of the accident but he'd flaked at the last minute. Not that his being there would have made a difference—or maybe it would have, maybe he would have gotten shot instead of, or as well as. No matter the scenario, Baby felt both guilty and relieved about not having been there, a mulched-up cowardice, no way to relate, nothing to say, so when his brother came home from the hospital and wanted to do nothing but game and smoke pot, who was he to tell him how to be?

Whenever his father tried to encourage Gobind to make a plan for the future, he would simply reply, "You don't know what it's like," and to that there was no comeback—not for any of them. Even when Baby tried to imagine what it must be like to not move your legs, to not feel anything, to sit in the same chair for most of the day, to need lifts, ramps and pullies to simply move from here to there, he could not.

Gobind chucked his headset across the room. "Fuck."

"Who were you playing with?"

"Some randoms."

Baby nodded.

"Don't judge."

"I'm not."

"Yeah, you are."

Baby raised his hands on either side of his head. "Whatever, man."

"Mom was looking for you."

"What's she want?"

"She needs you to clean out the spare room for Boston Auntie. She'll be here in a couple days." Gobind reached over and pinched his brother's cheek. "Ladoo, so handsome, my sweet sweet," he said, imitating the auntie's Bollywood British accent.

"Cut it out." Baby slapped Gobind's hand away.

"Apparently she's bringing Mottu with her."

"No way. Haven't seen her in ages. You guys still keep in touch?"

"No, but it'll be cool to see her again."

"I bet," Baby said, nudging his brother.

"You're such an idiot," he said and wheeled over to the bookcase, grabbing a joint from his stash.

"No way. Don't. Mom will be able to smell that shit."

"Nah, she's cooking in the garage with Masi. All she can smell is onions. She's totally curry blind by now. They've been at it all day."

Baby's phone buzzed. He clicked on the video link Devi had sent and waited for it to load.

Gobind handed him the joint.

"Nah, I'm good."

"Suit yourself," he said. "What are you watching anyway?"

"Devi sent the video thing for the reception."

"Put it on the screen," he said and tossed the remote to Baby. They both watched in silence for a few minutes, mouths gaping as the Bollywood-inspired trailer played.

FADE IN. PUNJABI MUSIC PLAYS.

Montage begins.

Ext. Dirt road, farm land, mid-afternoon.

Leather-clad Baby on a motorbike riding down a dirt road.

Devi wears a yellow salwar kameez, runs through the fields, fingertips touching long grass.

Devi gets on the back of the motorbike.

Cut to: Devi's hands around Baby's waist. Close-up shot of engagement ring. They ride off into the sunset, hair blowing in the wind.

Ext. Forest.

Baby and Devi walking through the trees toward each other.

Shy, Devi hides behind a tree.

Baby strums a guitar and walks toward her, serenading.

Ext. Beach at sunset.

Devi in blue sari walking in the surf, close-up of feet and ankle bracelets.

Baby, in wet T-shirt, splashes her.

Devi, modest, turns away.

Baby reaches for her, close-up on hands.

Int. Luxury hotel staircase.

Baby, in black tuxedo, watches Devi descend stairs.

Devi wears a red floor-length gown.

Baby reaches for her hand and kisses it.

Cut to: Devi and Baby toast champagne.

Fade to black.

THEY SAT IN STUNNED SILENCE UNTIL GOBIND SUDDENLY BURST INTO laughter. "What the fuck was that?"

Baby sighed, shaking his head. "I know. It's Devi. Her cousin in London did this instead of the usual slide show thing for her reception."

"Why?"

"Fuck if I know."

"It's not that bad."

"Really?"

"Sure, I mean you totally had the Shah Rukh Khan moment down. I think you even had a nipple shot."

"What?"

"The beach scene. The wet T-shirt."

"No way."

"Yeah way. Play it again."

"No, we are not watching it again."

"Come on. This is the most I've laughed all day." Gobind took the remote from Baby and pressed play. With the joint pursed between his lips, he lifted and twisted his hands to the bhangra beat. After watching the video two more times, Gobind, good and stoned, paused it on a shot of Baby on the motorbike looking longingly into the camera. "This is epic."

"Epic fail."

"Not gonna lie bro, it's super cheesy."

Baby leaned back into the couch cushions, his hands over his face. "How am I gonna tell her?"

"You just gotta tell her it's not your thing, it's not you."

"Yeah, It's just not me," Baby said, repeating it twice, practising.

THE FOLLOWING EVENING, BABY PARKED HIS CAR NEAR ONE OF THE outbuildings to avoid having to talk to Devi's family, just as he'd done before her parents knew they were dating, back when they thought she just spent a lot of time at the library and out for coffee with friends. Things were no-pressure simple before either set of parents knew, but like with all Indian parents, once they did, things were set in motion. Even though their parents said things like "Times have changed," proclaiming modernity, the community had not changed much, and What will people say? was still a question that demanded a ring.

Their families should have been happy with the match, a union of two good families, albeit Devi's family claimed to be the better of the two, given their money and alleged historic claims to Canada; they had family on the *Komagata Maru*. The Dosanjhs—so they liked to say—paved the way for other Indians to come to Canada, Indians like the Atwals. The way Devi's grandmother had said it made Baby believe he and his family, with their humble beginnings, were supposed to be grateful.

"Don't listen to her, Baby," Devi had said after the families first met. "She's just an old woman who's used to having her way."

"Sounds like someone else I know," Baby had said, laughing when she mock-slapped him. But now, as he thought of all the drama since, he wondered if he was right and that Devi was more like her dadi than she liked to admit. Had he mistaken her entitlement for confidence?

Lately, he was struggling hard to remember who they'd been without this wedding. Ever since they'd set a date she'd become an octopus, always reaching for something, always asking for something—when before, just being together was enough. He couldn't remember the last time they'd gone to see a movie or eaten a meal without their phones on the table. It started with brief stints on Pinterest, Instagram and TikTok, but now her social feeds were a full-time thing, her wedding posts garnering so much interest that she'd started thinking about becoming a professional influencer. "I do have a marketing degree. This could be my job," she'd said when he told her that her constant post, share and click-here life was making him feel like a content prop.

Had she been anyone else, he might have broken it off, but now it felt too late; he'd invested too much time and his parents had invested more money than they could afford. Sometimes he felt like he was being dragged along by a rushing current, grabbing at whatever he could get hold of, including parts of life that were meant for Gobind. Baby hadn't wanted to be a doctor, but he hadn't *not* wanted to be a doctor either. It's just that he hadn't decided on anything and then had somehow inherited Gobind's decisions. At times, he thought he was only getting married because Gobind's intended had ended their relationship. After the accident, she'd said that being with him was too hard and that she hoped he didn't think she was a terrible person— and because he wasn't a terrible person, he'd said he understood. Gobind mistook her deficiency for his own and hadn't been with anyone since. When Baby started dating Devi, Gobind was surprised; for his whole adult life, Baby had been low-key in love with Anne Liu. Her parents ran the Chinese restaurant where Baby worked and they'd been best friends since their first year of university. It was obvious to everyone who knew them that though they weren't dating, they should have been. After meeting Devi for the first time, Gobind asked Baby what he liked about Devi and he couldn't say. Looking back now, he realized he should have known that was a sign.

With the wedding drawing closer, most of Baby's conversations with Devi ended in tense full-stop sentences that came close to ultimatums. In those moments he tried to remember what he loved about her, and even now, as she was running toward him in the rain, he thought hard about it but realized there was nothing really special about her. She wasn't that smart or funny, and without her makeup she was plain, her nose too long, her lips too thin and her eyes too far apart, her entire face an abstraction. Was that part of what attracted him? The non-specialness, the cubist face, the way she didn't fit together but was interesting to study and to look at—not beautiful— just curious enough to hold his attention, like some weird painting. He hated that he thought this. He hated that the wedding stress was making him think this way. He reminded himself that he loved her.

She tried the door and then tapped on the glass.

"Sorry, sorry," he said as he opened the door. "I thought it was unlocked."

"It's so fucking miserable out," she said, as she slid into the car. "It better not rain on our day. It'll ruin everything. Did your dad get the tents? The planner is looking for some extra ones for us just in case. But I want the ones with the windows and clear roof and she doesn't know if she can get them, but I told her to try harder, because I don't want my guests packed into a circus tent." As Devi went on about the weather and the wedding, Baby watched the way she ran her fingers through her damp hair, pulling out knots. How absorbed she was in everything she was saying, like she actually believed it mattered.

"I'm sure it'll be fine," he said, reaching for her hand.

"You think?"

"For sure."

43

"Thanks," she said, her eyes narrowing. "I needed to hear that." She leaned in and kissed him, once and then again. "I miss you. It's been too long. I miss us," she said and before he knew it, she had taken off her top and was kissing his neck, telling him all the things she wanted to do to him. She pulled down his zipper.

"Whoa, whoa, slow down," he said between kisses.

"What? What's wrong?" Her body was leaning into his, her hand pressing into his crotch.

"Nothing's wrong. I just thought we should talk."

"Talk," she said, taken aback. "Are you mad at me or something?"

"Why would I be mad?"

"Fuck, I knew it." She yanked her hand away and pulled her T-shirt back on. "You're still mad about Vegas. I told you already nothing happened with Jessie."

"God, that was months ago," Baby said, trying not to react to Devi's routine button pushing. She knew that he hated Jessie, but she'd never asked him why and he hadn't told her; that was between him and Gobind. "Besides, whatever happens in Vegas stays in Vegas, right?"

"Right, exactly. I didn't ask you about your stag, or about why Anne was there, did I?"

"Well you actually did, but—"

"Are you serious right now?"

He sighed, pressing his head back into the leather rest, unsure of what to say.

"So what are you mad about then? Dadi wanting to pay for the wedding?"

"I don't know what you're talking about."

"I told my dadi about your dad driving the taxi, so she called your mom and offered to help out."

"She didn't."

"She did. I'm sorry. I didn't think it would be a big deal. Besides, your mom turned her down."

"Of course she did." Baby shook his head. "Your grandmother is unbelievable."

"No, unbelievable is that your mom insisted on a dowry."

"What? No, it's not a dowry. Devi, we talked about this; it was practically your idea. It's like you said, it's money to help us get on our feet."

"I just don't see the difference. The money my parents are giving us is to help us, and the money my dadi was trying to give your parents is to help them. I didn't think you'd be mad about it."

"Mad about it? I didn't even know about it."

"Then why are you so upset? Is your mom still pissed about the sweets?"

"No, but you have to admit your family using a different sweet shop was pretty shady."

"Well, they only did that after the dowry business."

"Would you stop calling it a dowry?"

"Fine," she said, crossing her arms over her chest.

"Look, let's not let our parents' issues get in the way."

"Okay." She nodded emphatically. "So, if it's not that, then what is it?"

Baby took a breath and put his hands on the wheel. "I don't know. The whole wedding. I guess it's getting to me. I just . . . I don't know."

"What do you mean you don't know? The wedding is less than two weeks away. Is this about us? Are you seriously getting cold feet?" She was staring at him, her face twisted.

"No," he said. "That's not it. It's . . . that wedding trailer. It put me off is all. It's just too much, Devi. It's all too much."

45

"I knew it. I knew you'd hate it," she said, shaking her head.

"Well, if you knew I'd hate it, why did you ask me to do it?"

"Because it's what people are doing now. No one does those old-school slide shows anymore."

"I like slide shows."

"Of course you do."

"What's that supposed to mean?"

"You're basic," she said, crossing her arms over her chest. "Everyone says so. Basic Baby."

"You used to like that I was simple."

"Big difference between simple and basic."

"Nice. See, this is exactly what I mean about you lately. Sometimes when you're talking, I don't even know who you are."

"I see," she said, her tone biting. "So this is about me."

"No. It's about us."

"Sounds like you're not even sure there *is* an us." She opened the car door and stepped out.

"I didn't say that, you did," he yelled, leaning over the passenger seat as she slammed the door in his face. She stood there on the other side of the rain-strewn glass for a moment, but to Baby she was just a blur. When she started walking away he should have followed her, told her to wait, to stop, to come back, but he didn't. He leaned back, head in hands, unsure of what had happened. He hadn't meant to upset her. He hadn't meant to say the things he'd said, but to whom else could he have said them?

NO THRU ROAD

SATNAM HAD BEEN DRIVING IN CIRCLES. THE TAXI QUEUE, ALREADY full with cabbies anticipating the onslaught of international arrivals, forced him to circumnavigate the airport for fifteen minutes. As he on-ramped and off-ramped his way through the terminal loops, he berated himself for not having arrived earlier. Had it not been for Balbir, her incessant list giving and reminders of all that he had yet to do for the wedding, he would have been on time. Satnam tried to put his wife out of his mind, yet there she was every few minutes, rattling around in the back of his head, a migraine of inadequacies—his and hers. Did she not see how hard he was working, toiling at the shop for eight hours, driving for ten and sleeping only when the fatigue was greater than his worries? He glanced at the top of his balding head in the rear-view mirror. "Waheguru," he said, pulling into an open spot in the queue. He had a habit of saying this every time something went his way, an acknowledgement of God in the moment. He closed his eyes and listened to the kirtan on the radio, humming along with the devotional song.

He hadn't been a religious person before the accident. Though he'd believed in God and had gone to the gurdwara regularly, he hadn't dwelt on the meaning of life; he was too busy for philosophy, too practical for theology. That changed after the accident; suddenly the day-to-day of the sweet shop and of raising a family seemed so pointless, and once Gobind returned home from the hospital—much to Balbir's dismay—Satnam went to India. Unlike his past trips that focused on the upkeep of their ancestral land, this trip was a pilgrimage. The night his son was shot, he'd sat in the hospital chapel and prayed, promising that if his son lived, he too would be born again. Although he explained all of this to Balbir, she was unmoved and when he set out to Hemkund Sahib, the star-shaped gurdwara set on a glacial lake high in the Himalayas, she didn't even wish him luck. Due to the terrain and altitude, the temple was only accessible for a few months each year, and it was there in the mountains that he found peace. After eating langar, he sat by the lake and closed his eyes, listening to the hollow winds that reminded him of the temporal nature of life. But somehow when he descended from the mountaintop, when he returned to the noise of his village, the lesson was gone, replaced by life's burdensome nature. That night when he slept, he dreamt that the elusive snow leopard who lived near Hemkund Sahib came into his home and lay down by the fire, the flames glinting in his amber eyes. When he told his cousin about this dream, his cousin said it was a sign and referred him to a holy man. Satnam had expected this man to be a swami of sorts, the type of bad actor one sees in a Hindi movie, with a white beard, saffron robes and wooden beads, but this man was entirely different. He looked like an accountant—sensible shoes, grey slacks and a cotton short-sleeved button-down shirt so thin that his undershirt showed through. The man had a trim hairstyle, gelled and parted to the side. His face was shiny, as if he had just applied lotion, and his entire demeanour was a mouse-like apology. Instead of rolling open scrolls, as Satnam had expected, the man pulled a laptop from his leather case and showed him maps of the sky, trigonometry-like charts and mathematical equations. "Put simply, sir," he finally said, "you have entered a seven-year cycle of upheaval. Things will improve for you only when the cycle is complete."

The cycle was now almost complete. October 17, 2022 was the date he was given, a date that he counted down to the way his children, when they were young, counted down the days until Christmas. He didn't tell his wife any of this; she wouldn't have believed him. She didn't believe in much and was about as thoughtful as a pounding fist, always reducing their lives to balance sheets and bill payments, the cost of living. They had just taken out a second mortgage on the house to finance their venture into frozen sweets when Baby had announced his plans to marry. Satnam had tried to coax him to wait, in hopes that the upheaval cycle would end and usher in a new era of prosperity buoyed by their business expansion, but Baby had insisted, so Satnam had taken to driving his cousin's taxi to help pay for the mounting debt. At last sum, their share of the wedding expenses was $250 thousand. Whenever he thought of it, his world fogged up the same way his glasses did when it was cold. He tried not to dwell on it, tried not to mention the strain to Baby who, being the good boy he was, worked part-time and helped out as best he could.

Had it not been for Devi and her family, the wedding would have been modest, a temple wedding, a reception in a community hall, the other events at home, celebrated with close family. But perhaps they weren't entirely to blame; it was the entire

Punjabi community that had gone mad, with their show and pomp, their need to outdo each other. He shook his head just thinking about the absurdity. Twenty thousand dollars for an elephant! That was one of the few times he'd said no, and he could see the relief on Baby's face when he struck down the idea. His son would not be riding an elephant to the gurdwara.

As he sat in the queue, he watched weary passengers line up at the roped-off taxi stand and wondered which would be his next fare—the Chinese family with two carts of expensive luggage, the white girl with dreadlocks and a backpack or the tall man with a carry-on—he wondered where they'd been, and made up stories that would likely prove far more interesting than the real ones turned out to be. People were mostly silent now, preferring the quiet to taxi small talk; they usually stared at their phones. Sometimes they asked about the weather or commented on the traffic, but no one looked out the window anymore. But even this was better than the downtown route, where drunk young people Baby's age would end up in the back of his cab after a night of partying, engaging in all kinds of lewd behaviour as if he wasn't even there and then pretending to be offended if they saw his eyes flicker in the rear-view. "Pervert, keep your eyes on the road. Fucking Paki!" That's what a young man who'd had his hands up his girlfriend's skirt had yelled at him the other night. "Sorry, sir. I was only watching the road," he'd said and it was true. He was a good driver and followed the rules: shoulder checks, signalling, yielding, stopping at yellow lights, never speeding ahead. He followed the rules, but what had it gotten him? Sometimes he wondered. While it was true what the white people said about time flying, for him the having fun part did not apply. For him time disappeared like part of a magic trick, like those beautiful boxed women in sparkling costumes who were sawed in half, their legs dangling merrily, their heads bobbing happily, seemingly unaware that they were no longer whole. But unlike those extraordinary women, he wasn't in on the trick and couldn't put himself back together.

He'd had dreams once, even if he now couldn't remember quite what they were, and reminded himself that he wasn't old enough for bitterness and forgetting; at only fifty-six, he had much to be grateful for, and every time he felt sorrow, he remembered the climb to the temple, the uphill trek, the air so thin it broke him open. Unlike others who'd gasped like fish out of water, who'd hired mules to carry them up, he'd forged ahead. Forward, his father used to say. God put your eyes on the front of your head for a reason. No looking back.

He drove, inching ahead as passengers loaded into the other taxis, and waited for his fare to approach. After Satnam placed the luggage in the trunk, the man thanked him and then much to his surprise, shook his hand and said, "Sat Sri Akal Paaji," before getting into the back of the car. He had never been greeted by a white man in his own language, nor had a white man ever called him *brother*, and as he pulled away from the curb, he felt nervous and excited all at once. He turned the radio down to an almost inaudible level. "Your Punjabi is very good, sir."

The man looked up from the newspaper he'd taken out of his briefcase. "My wife is Indian," he said, putting his paper down. Satnam noted he had a warm smile and that put him at ease. "When our sons were young, she spoke to them in Punjabi. I'm afraid I may remember more of it than they do."

"How old are your children, if I may ask?"

"Twenty and twenty-five."

Satnam's eyes widened, surprised that this man was likely not much younger than himself and yet there was something energetic about him, something magnetic, as if he represented all Satnam could want or hope for. The man leaned forward, his arm extending over Satnam's shoulder as he showed him a photo in his wallet. "Ash and Anik. Ash is the younger one," he said, pointing him out. By the way the man was smiling, Satnam could tell that Ash was the man's favourite, and wondered if it was because he looked more like his father. Satnam had tried hard not to favour Gobind but he couldn't help himself. He was everything a father could have asked for in a son.

"Handsome young men," he remarked.

"I take no credit. They look like my wife." The man smiled again and tucked his wallet into his breast pocket.

"I have two sons also."

"Oh yeah? How old?"

"Twenty-seven and twenty-nine. My youngest just finished medical school. He's getting married next weekend."

"Congratulations. You must be so proud."

"We are," Satnam said and for a moment he forgot his troubles and grinned, quietly satisfied with his life, this validation that he should feel proud. Glancing back he noted that the man was looking out the window. Out the window! He knew this man was different from the others. Up ahead the traffic came to a crawl. "Sorry, sir."

"That's Vancouver traffic for you. Please call me Peter."

"Peter," he repeated. "My name is Satnam."

"Satnam—the true name, I am truth."

"Yes, sir. I mean, Peter," he said, impressed with this man who knew the meaning of his name, this man who called him brother, this man who looked out the window when so many others would have sat cradling their phones.

Satnam tuned the radio to the news and traffic station. There had been an accident and the southbound lanes of the bridge were closed. There was no way to turn back.

Peter opened one of the complimentary water bottles that Satnam had placed in the arm rest at the start of his shift. "So tell me, how long have you been a taxi driver?"

"Oh no, I'm just doing a favour for a friend," he said, suddenly embarrassed by his situation and desperate for Peter to think better of him than just as the nice Indian cabbie who gave complimentary bottled water. "Actually, my family and I run a sweet shop and restaurant. Maybe you know it? Baby Nanak's Sweet Shop."

"Know it? Hell, my wife loves your barfi! Tell me, what's the secret ingredient that makes it so creamy?"

Satnam laughed. "If I told you, it wouldn't be a secret."

"Well my friend, that is some business you've got. Congratulations."

"Thank you." Satnam thought to tell Peter about his new venture in frozen sweets but stopped himself. He didn't want to tempt the evil eye, especially since his seven-year cycle was not over. "And you, you're coming back from a business trip?"

"Yes, I was teaching in Toronto."

"You are a professor?" he asked.

"No, a life coach." Peter handed Satnam a business card.

Satnam glanced at the card and tucked it into his shirt pocket. "A life coach?"

"Yes, it's someone who helps people with their problems."

"I see, like a psychiatrist, or a psychologist."

"Not quite. I'm not a medical doctor and I don't work with patients."

Satnam nodded, remembering the family counselling session they'd had after Gobind's accident, the endless talk of feelings that made the room quiet and heavy. He and his wife had had so little to say, and in this way they were the same, careful not to say things that could not be unsaid, careful not to give the shapeless things a name. "So, like a therapist?"

"Not exactly. A life coach helps people focus their energy on setting and achieving goals. It's action oriented." He leaned forward, animatedly. Peter was a hand talker, conducting and directing the conversation. "When I work with people, I help them see what's in their way, what might be blocking them, and together we create a plan to help them. Therapy is more focused on mental health."

"Interesting," Satnam said, still pondering. "So you coach people on how to live?"

"I suppose I do," Peter said.

"And you studied this in school?"

"No. Actually I was a lawyer, practising family law, mostly divorce. But it was then that I realized there was a pattern to people's unhappiness and that maybe I could help them. You see, most people get divorced because they never knew how to love themselves; if they can't accept themselves, how can they love another?"

"And you teach this?"

"Yes, among other things."

"You are a wise man," Satnam said, flattering him in that deferential way that he'd come to realize people expected of immigrants. "People today are consumed by themselves. Faithless. But you—you help them see beyond their limitations. In that manner of speaking, today's life coach is yesterday's spiritual man."

"Maybe. Hmm. I never thought of it that way."

"Wisdom and faith for the non-believers." Satnam paused. "You give people hope that their lives can change, you give them purpose. This coaching, this self-help, is to them what religion is to others—a guide."

"Well, I try to avoid religious rhetoric."

"Oh I see, you are not a man of faith?" There was an awkward silence. "Sorry. I didn't mean to offend or overstep."

"You did neither," he said, thoughtfully. "I don't know what I believe exactly . . . But I don't disbelieve. Agnostic, I suppose."

"I was like that. Agnostic. But then, God came to me in my suffering. My son, my eldest, he was badly hurt in an accident, and I asked God, Why? Why have you done this to me?"

"And what did God say?"

"Nothing. God does not speak, he only reveals. Some time later, I went to India and prayed in a very remote mountain temple, and there it became clear to me that God is just the name we lend to hope."

Peter shook his head and slapped his knee. "You see, Satnam—you are your name!"

Satnam beamed and tilted his head as if to say, Of course.

"I travelled to India after college," Peter told him. "Amazing place," he said, reminiscing about Goa's party scene and Mumbai's slums, the way all tourists did.

"Is that where you met your wife?"

"Oh no, I didn't meet Pavan until years later. She runs a housekeeping service called Clean and Tidy." Peter handed him another business card. "In case you ever need someone."

"Thank you," Satnam said, quickly inspecting it before placing it in the cupholder. "You have a very successful family."

"Kind of you to say," Peter said and stared out the window as they passed one of the Blueberry King billboards.

Satnam had grown to hate those silly signs with their "Eat like royalty" slogan, a constant reminder of his future daughter-in-law's frivolity, her big business idea, her claim to fame, a rebranding of her family's blueberry farms. She was not worthy of his son, not worthy at all, but what could he do? Nothing. Children didn't listen to their parents anymore, not like when he was young. "Tell me," Satnam began, glancing back at Peter who was now looking at him, or looking ahead, it was hard to tell. "Do your children listen to your life coaching?"

"Listen? Yes. Heed? Not so much," he said, laughing softly.

"That's just the way it is then. Fathers and sons."

"It is. But I do think they listen; I think they listen more than we give them credit for; I know I did." His eyes softened. "I listened to everything my dad ever said; I didn't mean to, but now as I get older he's just there, a voice in my head telling me what to do. Just last week, I was working in the yard, fixing some fence boards that had come loose, and there he was in my head, telling me how to do it. His voice was so clear that for a minute I thought he was standing right next to me."

"Your father, he must have been a good man."

"Yeah, he was." A pause. "He tried real hard," he said, smiling in a slightly pained way as he looked out the window.

For a time, Satnam looked back at Peter, waiting for an encouragement to talk some more, but when no such invitation came, Satnam returned his focus to the road ahead.

Peter lived in a cedar house on a treed lot in the hills. The house, with only two garages, was not as large as Satnam's, and the front door not as grand as Satnam's stone-arched entryway, but the neighbourhood, with its meandering streets and cul-de-sacs was peaceful in a way that Satnam's neighbourhood, only twenty minutes away, was not: no clothes lines in the backyard, no basement suites, no street parking; no cheap lawn ornaments, no cooking smells, no loud voices. Here there was no one that did not belong. Even the street signs said No Thru Road.

"Thank you," Peter said as Satnam pulled his luggage from the trunk.

Satnam folded his hands. "Sat Sri Akal Paaji."

Peter pressed a twenty-dollar bill into Satnam's palm. "You take care."

"You also." Satnam meant to tell Peter to come to the sweet shop sometime, to bring his wife, that he'd give him a discount, but he didn't say any of these things; instead he watched Peter unlock his door and enter the dimly lit house.

As Satnam drove away, around the traffic-calming round-about, down the treed lanes toward the highway, he wondered if Peter's wife was waiting for him, if his children would greet him, if they would have a family dinner.

On the way back to the airport Balbir called, and since he had no fare, he put the phone on speaker, only half paying atten-tion as she reminded him to pick up his suit from the cleaners, go to the bank and get her jewellery from the safety deposit box, go to Costco to get butter and milk, go, go, go, go. He said yes to everything.

As Balbir's tinny voice filled the cab, Satnam felt for Peter's business card in his pocket, touching its edges as if it were a talis-man, thinking about what Peter had said about setting goals and actions, a plan for life even when life has other plans. He thought of the small apartment above their first sweet shop, their hum-ble and happy beginnings; but whether they were actually happy, he couldn't say for certain. The past and present were stacked up against each other, a side-by-side comparison, a thumb on one side of the scale or the other, depending on who was doing the weighing. He wondered what Peter would tell him about his life, what obstacle he would find, what plan he would make to help Satnam achieve his goals—of what, exactly? Peace?

The sun was setting and the last of its light cut across the windshield, blinding Satnam momentarily. He pulled the visor down and squinted hard, narrowing his focus. "I have to go," he said to his wife, and hung up. He tuned the radio to Gurbani Kirtan 24-7 and slowed down as he signalled right toward the off-ramp. The black suv that had been tailgating him for a few kilometres honked and zipped around him. Satnam did not make eye contact even though he knew the other man was shouting at him. He let the space between them grow until the driver, satisfied with his level of torment, sped away. He knew that type of person, angry and wild, the very type of person that in some rage pulled the trigger that had paralyzed his son, the type of person so desperate to belong, to be noticed. The type of person he had tried so hard not to be, tried so hard not to raise. His boys were good boys. They didn't ride around in Escalades with tinted windows. No matter what the police had tried to insinuate, what had happened to Gobind was not his fault; he was a good student, a good son, and would never have gotten mixed up with the wrong people—much less a gang. "No, he barely knew this Jessie person," Satnam told them, and to suggest otherwise was too much. Had they not been through enough? "Wrong place, wrong time, innocent bystander." That's what Gobind and all the eye witnesses had told the police. No one was ever charged.

Sometimes in the middle of the night Satnam woke up wondering what would become of Gobind. At first, when Gobind came home from the hospital, Satnam had just wanted his son to be comfortable—they had made adjustments to the house so he could move around without bumping into walls. They had widened doorways, lowered counters, added ramps and lifts—anything to remove life's daily obstacles—but Satnam could see now, after having talked to Peter, that Gobind's day-to-day living was not the same as Gobind having a life. He wondered if God had put Peter in his path for this very reason. He took the business card out of his pocket and needled it into his wallet so as not to lose it.

As he drove into the muted twilight, he looked in the rear-view mirror, catching shades of himself each time. His eyes dimmed as he remembered what Peter had said about his father. "He tried real hard."

"Yes, he did," Satnam said, locking his eyes on the road. "Yes, he did."

READY FOR THIS JELLY?

T EN DAYS BEFORE HER WEDDING, SITTING IN FRONT OF THE STUDIO'S backlit mirror, makeup pots, pallets and tubes scattered in front of her, Devi's thoughts were elsewhere. Whether on her to-do list or otherwise, she could not exactly say; all she knew was that sitting in the white swivel chair and staring at her reflection in the three-way mirror made her feel as if she were in a fun house, and her mind bounced between images, unable to decide which version of herself to settle on. She stared straight ahead at her unmade face, her long hair pulled back tight, the blank canvas of herself, and tried to remember the last time she had been so plain and free. She rarely left the house without at least the essentials of brow, mascara and gloss, the bare-face makeup trend that made her aspire to be a ten-years-younger, freshly washed version of herself.

She'd loved makeup since she was a five-year-old girl sitting on the porcelain-tiled bathroom floor, her back against the oyster-shaped Jacuzzi, playing with her dadi's cosmetics. Cartoon-faced, she'd stared at herself in the small gold compact and her mother—who had come upon the scene—had laughed and taken a photo of her. Later, when that compact went missing and her dadi asked her if she knew of its whereabouts, Devi insisted she didn't, and even though everyone understood she had taken it, they pretended not to. Her family was masterful in their pretending.

They'd been pretending her father wasn't an alcoholic for as long as she could remember. When she was little, she just knew it as the way he was—angry, tired, sullen. His moods were something to be protected from and whenever he came home in a rage her brother, Gurjot, would tell her to run and hide. Two years her senior, Jot understood what was happening, but rather than explaining it he made it part of their hide-and-seek, excusing their parents' shouting as part of the game. She had to stay hidden until it was quiet. Once, after hiding in the closet under the stairs for over an hour, Devi came out, peeked into the kitchen and saw her brother helping their mother up off the ground. She went back to her hiding place and waited, but no one came. The next morning, her mother's eye was a patchwork of green and blue, and Devi, sitting on the bathroom counter, stick legs dangling, watched as her mother layered concealer on her face. When Devi asked why she was doing that, her mother said, "To look beautiful, of course," and playfully dabbed cream onto her daughter's nose. No one besides Jot came to her mother's rescue; everyone pretended not to know, and in those last few years when her father became too ill to be a tyrant, when the doctors could no longer medicate him into better health and his kidneys had given out, it was her mother who took care of him. She tended to his daily needs, took him to his specialist appointments, while Dadi and Jot managed the farm. Her father had run it into the ground, racked up debt, borrowed against it, and according to her dadi, had it not been for Devi's grandfather's real estate investments the family would have been ruined. Years ago, when Jot had asked their mother, "Why, after everything, do you stay?" She told him, "What choice did I have?" She'd been standing at the kitchen sink drying dishes, and she'd said it without looking up from her task; she'd put it as plainly as if she was remarking on the weather, as if her answer to his question was that it was not a question at all. Devi had been eighteen at the time, old enough to resent her mother and vow to never fall into the trap of becoming her. Aside from her dadi, the women in her family were mostly forgotten pushover-type women and for good reason. In her family, wealth did not pass from father to daughter—only from father to son. She suspected that she—like her grandfather's sister, Jasvir—would receive nothing in the end. Although Jot assured her otherwise, she saw how money changed people, how it made them hard. She loved that Baby wasn't like that, and she couldn't wait to be married and out of her parents' home. But in the meantime she acted the part of a good daughter in the family charade and took whatever she felt entitled to. Anytime her father complained about her extravagant spending, the wedding costs, the dowry she'd convinced Baby to ask for, she was secretly thrilled. He owed her at least that much.

While waiting for Jag to arrive, Devi grabbed a magazine from the nearby stack, gleaning the headlines: "Abs in 21 Days," "Red Hot Sex," "What He Wants You to Know" and "Lose 10 pounds in 1 Month." She flipped pages ferociously, glancing only at the photos and bold type before tossing the magazine back on the pile. She wandered over to the floor-to-ceiling arched windows, her heels clicking on the reclaimed hardwood. The seventeenth-floor Yaletown studio was spare and modern—exposed ductwork, cement counters, brick and beams passing as structural—the kind of cool Devi could only aspire to. Outside it was grey and tired, and on the street below people looked so small that with her thumb on the glass she could crush them like ants. Her gauzy reflection hovered on the window and she took a deep breath as she stared through herself to the outside world, as though she were trying to find her place in it. "Everything is fine," she said in a half whisper, convincing herself the way same she did each morning with her mirror affirmations—distilled survival self-talk and power poses. *You've got this. Go get it, girl! Take what's yours.* By the time she'd started university, she'd become intentional about her future and made a vision board. She cut pictures out of *Vogue* and the wedding edition of *Awaaz*, pictures of designer clothing, wedding rings, tropical beaches, luxury cars, bridal clothes, abs and shirtless men from perfume ads. These men all looked similar—dark hair, chiselled jawlines and three-day stubble. Baby and the wedding was a manifestation of everything she'd ever wanted, and now she just wanted to get on with it.

Beyond the frosted partition she heard Jag laughing with another client and it made her envious that she wasn't in on the joke. *When is it going to be my turn?* The thought crossed her mind like tickertape and looped back again and again. In some ways her entire life had felt like a waiting game, waiting to get out, waiting to start her own life, and in a way her wedding was as much a celebration of that as it was of her actual marriage. Her life was finally about to start.

"What a surprise!" Jag sauntered in, running her hand through her cropped platinum hair, looking as if she'd just woken from a nap. "I wasn't expecting to see you before the big day." She swivelled the leather chair toward Devi like an invitation. "What's up?"

Devi sat down. "Where to begin? It's such a disaster," she said, twirling around to see herself in the mirror. Next to Jag with her dyed hair, nose ring, combat boots and vintage rock T-shirt, Devi looked boring and branded. Her Chanel belt alone was more expensive than Jag's entire second-hand, flea market–find wardrobe and yet Jag had the one thing Devi didn't, courage. Jag, the most sought-after stylist in the city, was a self-made, unmarried mother and entrepreneur who lived life on her own terms. When Jag had first mentioned her partner, Devi thought she meant her business partner and felt so foolish, so old-fashioned.

"Details?"

"Rosie's cousin Pinky used Hollywood glam as the theme for her reception," Devi said in one long exhale.

Jag, who was raking her fingers through Devi's hair the way stylists do, stopped and stared at their mirrored reflections. "No way."

Devi nodded. "Yep, everything. Hair, makeup, decorations. All of it."

"Coincidence?" she said, raking again.

"No way. Rosie said she didn't tell her, but what are the odds that someone has the exact same theme?"

"What are you going to do?"

"What *can* I do? I have to change it up." Devi took out her phone, handing it to Jag who swiped through her inspiration photos of movie stars from a bygone era. "Old Bollywood instead of Hollywood. What do you think?"

Jag gathered up Devi's hair, twisting it into a bun. "It could work. A low bun with a jasmine garland instead of the Veronica Lake wave, and then we go heavy with the earrings instead of pearls. We can keep the makeup matte, winged eyeliner, dark brows and a bold lip and bindi."

Devi, still staring at herself in the mirror, nodded. "Perfect."

"What about your outfit?"

"I think it can still work. I'm going for my final fitting after this and then I'll know if I need a backup outfit."

"A backup?"

"You can never be too prepared," Devi said, explaining the embroidery and beadwork on her lehenga.

"Okay then, let's give this a try." Jag twirled the chair around. For the next hour Jag ran brushes over Devi's face, contouring, concealing, highlighting, always taking a step back to admire and adjust before she added another layer. Refusing to let Devi see anything but the finished product, she then started in on her hair, heating and teasing, twisting and pinning, all with just the right amount of sprinkled small talk, mostly about the wedding. Jag was good at making her clients feel special, she was carefree and confident and it made Devi feel lucky to be in her care. Devi loved the attention, the same way she loved sitting, slightly elevated, in the massage chair at Eurospa in front of the Vietnamese girl who filed and painted her nails, the girl who did not speak English well and whose only words were "You choose colour." Devi went there once a month for her nails, and every other month to be steamed, exfoliated and massaged. Giselle at reception knew Devi by name and always had a glass of sparkling wine waiting for her in the dressing room. There she'd slip on a plush robe, listen to the soothing ambient soundtrack, and sip her drink while she waited for the aesthetician. Once, she took her mom there for Mother's Day, but Raman, a modest person, did not like to be touched, and couldn't understand how Devi let these starch-uniformed women rub their hands all over her as if they were skinning and tenderizing meat. Devi wasn't able to explain that the quiet intimacy of self-care made her feel whole, real even.

"So this Rosie girl, isn't she in your wedding party?" Jag asked, pinning Devi's hair. "Tell me if it's too tight."

Devi nodded that it was fine. "She is. We used to be best friends when we were little kids," she said, recounting the Destiny's Child dance-offs they'd have in her room, belting out all the wrong lyrics to "Bootylicious," jiggling their behinds and singing about what jelly could and could not be handled. Sometimes they'd argue over who got to be Beyoncé. "I thought about kicking her out of the wedding party but it's drama either way. If I take her out, she freaks and does who knows what, and on top of that we'd be short on the bridesmaids-to-groomsmen ratio. But if I leave her in—sure, it's awkward, but at least the pictures will look good." Devi reached for a bottle of sparkling water. "I should have known not to trust her; she's been weird ever since she got married last year, and then," Devi said, shaking her head, "in Vegas she was a mess the entire time."

"At your girls' weekend?"

"Yes, can you believe it? It was my weekend and somehow she made it about her, and then . . ." she paused. "Never mind, I shouldn't say."

"Come on, spill the chai."

Devi looked around to make sure no one was nearby and whispered, "So one night we're in a club, having a good time and she up and disappears with some guy. We end up looking for her all night and get separated in the process. I bump into Jessie, one of my brother's friends from high school—who I hadn't seen in ages—and he agrees to help me look for her. Jessie and I spent the entire night walking along the strip, going into casinos and clubs looking for her and then the next day Rosie shows up at brunch, still hungover, hickeys on her neck, acting like nothing happened."

Jag halo-sprayed Devi's hair. "Crazy."

"It gets crazier because when we get back from Vegas, Rosie tells everyone that I hooked up with Jessie."

"No!" Jag puts the hairspray bottle down for effect.

"Yes! Can you believe it? The nerve, right?"

"Nuts."

"I mean, here I am, looking for her, and basically she stabs me in the back and now everyone thinks that Jessie and I had a thing, which of course we didn't."

"Why would she say that?"

"I asked her the same thing and she said she'd seen us in a casino playing slots and drinking which, yes, we had been, but only while looking for her. Crazy, right? It's like she was projecting what she did onto me or something."

"So *did* anything happen with this Jessie guy?"

"No, no," Devi said, dismissing the idea as absurd, even though she'd had a crush on Jessie all throughout high school and had doodled his name in hearts all over her notebooks. At sixteen, she'd spent hours imagining their wedding, practising her *Mrs. Bhatti* signature and thinking how perfect Devinder Bhatti sounded. For a time, he was all she ever thought about, and now, having spent time with him again, all those feelings had returned. "It was totally PG. We just walked along the strip all night, talking about old times, looking for Rosie." Devi shook her head, trying not to think of it, of him anymore. It was true, they had just talked, but it was easy in a way that talking to Baby hadn't been these last few months. They talked about growing up, their fucked-up families and what they wanted their futures to be. Unlike Baby who had grown up with decent parents, Jessie understood what it was like to live in an unstable home, how it changed you and made you scared and fierce all at once. When the night grew colder, he, like a perfect gentleman, took his jacket off and placed it around her shoulders. It was the kind of night that was full of nostalgia and anticipation; she knew that something could have happened, but nothing did. They exchanged phone numbers but didn't call. They followed each other on Instagram, hearting posts as if it meant something. For weeks after, she thought of texting him at least a few times every day, drafting clever and breezy messages in her head that she never dared to send—until last month. As soon as she hit send, as soon as she saw her *Been thinking about you* text in the blue bubble, she wished she could have unsent it. But then came the three dots, and her regret was replaced with relief; he felt the same way. She told herself it was a harmless flirty exchange, a first-love fantasy, a way to work out the wedding jitters, that no one would ever know, and that even if they did, she could say they were just friends—but what kind of friends send pics? She didn't have an answer for that. She should never have sent it.

"What does Baby think about it?"

Devi was startled, and for a moment wondered if Jag had read her guilty mind.

"Oh, lucky for me, everyone knows that Rosie is batshit and all the other girls backed me up. Besides, Baby isn't the jealous type." Sometimes she wished that he was and even blamed his lack of passion for her own actions. If he were more dominant, more aggressive, more controlling or just *more* in general, then maybe she wouldn't be getting off over late-night video calls with Jessie.

What she needed was a good stress fuck. When she offered herself up to Baby the other night in his car, he turned her down. Hurt, she picked a fight with him, blaming him for all their drama when she knew it was all her fault. He'd never wanted anything from her family but she'd convinced him to ask for the money. She wanted her share. She deserved that. She deserved more. *I am worthy.* It was another one of her affirmations.

As Jag finished her hair, Devi picked up the *Awaaz* magazine and flipped to the Dear Auntie column, which was so staid compared to the other Dear Auntie that had blown up online. Guilt having gotten the better of her, Devi had DMed the new Dear Auntie from a fake account, asking for advice on what do about having feelings for someone else when you're about to get married. It was a stupid question with only a few possible answers—most of which involved coming clean, telling the truth and calling off the wedding—none of which she was willing to do. "He deserves to know the truth," is what Dear Auntie had posted. Hundreds of followers commented and liked her advice but Devi did not. Baby did not deserve the truth. He deserved better.

"Almost done." Jag stepped back to admire Devi like a work of art. "Ready?" She twirled her toward the mirror. "What do you think?"

Devi stared at herself for a moment and then reached back and lightly touched her hair, the flowers.

"We'll use a real garland for the reception, this is just a mock-up, and of course it will look better when you're dressed and have the right jewellery on. You should go really big on the earrings, and I'm thinking . . . a round red bindi," she said, and placed one on Devi's forehead.

As Jag continued to talk about the details, Devi stood up and examined her face from every angle. It was just as she'd hoped it would be. She looked timeless, like someone from a black and white era with poreless skin, kohl-lined cat eyes, lips filled in with a pomegranate red that Jag had mixed just for her. She didn't look like herself. "It's perfect," she said and took a mirror selfie.

"What time do you have to be at the fitting?"

Devi looked at her watch. "About an hour."

Jag handed her the makeup wipes and started pulling pins out of the updo. What took hours to create was undone in just minutes.

⁓

FANCY FASHIONS WAS THE FIRST AND LARGEST TEXTILE STORE ON MAIN Street. Like most of the shops on the Little India strip, it was utilitarian, with its wall-to-wall bolts of fabric and glass displays stuffed with colourful suits and saris that by midday would have been unfolded and left in heaps on the countertop. Window mannequins with blue eyeshadow, blonde hair and missing limbs donned the latest fashions, and out front the sidewalk was littered with rolling racks of last year's lineup at today's special prices. Devi would have preferred to shop at one of the exclusive appointment-only designer boutiques that had professional window displays, good lighting and change rooms that did not double as stockrooms, but her mother and grandmother both insisted on Fancy Fashions for their custom work, on-site alterations and long-standing relationships. Their families were from neighbouring villages. They were loyal that way.

The shop was in its usual state of disorder when Devi arrived. Although it had been open for hours, there were large boxes of new stock being unpacked, and somewhere someone was still vacuuming. Since she was early for her appointment, she perused the new line of clothing while watching a family haggle with the owner. Because nothing was priced, everyone, including the staff, had to ask Uncleji—who wasn't actually anyone's uncle—what the price was. Some would take the first offer but those who understood

70

the unspoken rules of haggling would push back and insist he do better, sometimes reminding him of their distant shared lineage. Uncleji's best price varied based on how much money a customer spent and how much he thought he would make on their referrals. He charged white people the most. They never haggled.

The only way to get the best price from Uncleji was to bring an elder with you, someone who was not embarrassed to raise their voice or feign insult, at which point Uncleji would pull out the small solar calculator he kept in his dress shirt and calculate a new sum. He never said the number out loud, just showed the customer the grey-scale figure while saying, "For you, this is the best price." Devi's dadi was masterful at this, and also at ensuring every garment was perfect. When they used the wrong gold thread on Devi's wedding lehenga and insisted it was the one they had chosen, it was her dadi that not only made them fix it but also made them discount it.

Devi wandered to the bridal section at the back of the shop. A few families were sitting on the leather couches oohing and aahing over a bride-to-be who had stepped onto the dressing room pedestal. Her baby-pink lehenga was covered in mirror-work and when she twirled she looked like a disco ball. Devi preferred a more traditional look. Her lehenga was red, hand embroidered with a Swarovski-inlaid border and had a double dupatta with a golden fringe. It was subtle and dramatic, a nod to royalty, inspired by the designer Sabyasachi but made just for her. She wanted to make sure she had something original.

"You're early," Suneet said, pulling a rolling rack behind her.

"Yeah, I was hoping to see the backup options you pulled for me."

"Sure, just give me a minute. I'm just finishing up with another client," she said, directing her attention to a group of customers—one of whom was Jessie Bhatti. Unlike Baby, who kept his hair long on top and wore sweats, Jessie was put together. His tight fade was highlighted by diamond studs and he was wearing an Armani T-shirt, a gold chain, designer jeans and trainers.

Devi hadn't seen him in real life since Vegas and though she'd imagined him in all kinds of ways, seeing him here wasn't one of them. She turned away and rummaged through a pile of saris on the nearby counter, pretending not to hear him when he called her name.

"I thought that was you," he said, now standing next to her.

"What are you doing here?" she whispered.

"My mom needed a ride. She's picking up her suit for the wedding."

"What wedding?"

"Uh, yours. We're invited, remember?" he said, trying to make eye contact.

"Right, of course." She pretended to look at one of the saris more closely. "My parents, they invited everyone."

"Oh, so now I'm everyone?" he asked, taking a step closer. "That's not what you said last night."

"You know what I mean," she said, still trying not to look at him. "You're my brother's friend. Our families know each other."

"And how about us? Do we know each other?" he said, his hand reaching for hers.

She smacked his hand. "Stop it," she said, louder than she meant to. "I'm getting married."

"I'm aware."

"Good. Just so we're clear." She took a step back and bumped into a mannequin, toppling it over.

Jessie bent down to help her pick it up. "Can I see you later?"

"No. You know I can't."

"I think you can," he said, as if it were a dare, before rejoining his group.

As Devi followed Suneet to the draped-off change rooms, she wondered if anyone had heard her talking to Jessie and if her mother would ask her about it when she got home. People talk—that's what her dadi always said, and she knew it was true. Devi loved a good piece of gossip; she just hated when it was about her, and hated it even more when it was true. She thought of her Dear Auntie post. She was wrong to say that she had feelings for someone else because now, having seen Jessie, she realized she didn't have feelings for him, she just had feelings. She was all mixed up, scared of being alone, scared of being invisible, scared of being seen, scared of settling down—just so goddamn scared. She wasn't ready. She never had been.

On her way home, she called Baby. They hadn't spoken since they'd fought the other night. They'd texted about wedding details but no one had said sorry, and after seeing Jessie, sorry was what she wanted to say most. A blanket apology for everything. He answered on the third ring and she was relieved to hear his voice, the depth of it. He was so easy, so self-assured.

"Hey, look," she said, aware that she was already grasping for the right words, that she was already screwing it up, "I just wanted to clear the air. I don't like how we left it the other night and I know we're just wedding stressed . . . so can we just forget about it?"

"Yeah, for sure," he said. "And, it's my bad. I should have told you how I felt about the trailer first."

"It's okay, we can scrap it and do a slide show."

"I thought you said that slide shows were basic."

"Nothing *I* do is basic. We can make it cool," she said.

73

"I appreciate that. Thanks."

"Of course." She was aware of how civil they were, how uncomplicated it could be. "I'm not far from your place. I could swing by and hang out."

"Maybe another time? Mom's got me cleaning out the guest room."

"Out-of-towners?"

"Yeah, Boston Auntie and my cousin Sonia."

"You don't have a cousin Sonia."

"They're family friends, you know how it is."

"Totally. So, is she cute?"

"Who, Sonia?"

"Yeah."

"I don't know. Haven't seen her for ages. She and Gobi were tight; I think our parents have been secretly planning their wedding since they were kids."

"Typical," Devi said, aware that her own mother and grandmother had lists of boys that would have been a good match for her, none of which were Baby, one of which had once been Jessie. "Well, I should let you get to it then. Call me later?"

"For sure. Talk soon."

"Hey Baby," she added. "Are we good?" By the time she asked, he'd already hung up, and when the phone rang again, she hoped it was him calling back—but it was Jessie asking to meet up.

She tried to say no, but she couldn't help herself. She never could.

BEST LAID
PLANS

THERE WAS NO ONE IN THE WORLD THAT JESSIE LOVED MORE THAN his eight-year-old niece, Amaya, and whenever his sister asked him to pick her up from school, he did so without hesitation. Like most little girls her age she loved arts and crafts, and together the two of them would watch episodes of *The Joy of Painting* on YouTube. Today, Jessie had surprised her with an easel and palette so she could follow along with the Bob Ross tutorial. As a kid, when a substitute art teacher played the PBS show as a time filler, Jessie thought it was hilarious that a white dude had an afro, but after watching again with Amaya, he could see the appeal. Bob Ross had a friendly Mister Rogers kind of voice that was creepy and comforting at the same time. Unlike all the men that Jessie knew who were calloused and tired, Bob was wise and kind in a grandfatherly way. He made painting look easy; in less than thirty minutes he could fill an empty canvas. He made mountains and trees with just a few clever brush strokes, and whenever he'd slip up he'd say that it wasn't a mistake, just a happy accident. Jessie wished that Bob was right and that there were no real mistakes in life, but as he glanced at his vibrating phone and saw the messages from Devi, he knew she was not a happy accident. She was definitely a mistake. He should never have fucked her. He hadn't planned on it, but like most things in his life, it just happened, and after it had, it seemed like it had been inevitable. When they'd met a few months ago, he was in Las Vegas for a friend's thirtieth birthday and he saw her alone on the strip looking slightly drunk and panicked. As a friend of her brother, Jot, he thought the right thing to do was to make sure she was okay and to get her back to her hotel safely, so he offered to help her find her missing friend. She was grateful and flirty the way girls are after they've mixed their liquor—loud and handsy with sleepy bedroom eyes. He knew she'd been in love with him since she was a kid and though he'd never thought of her that way, he liked that she liked him. She didn't see him the way other people did; she didn't see him as a player, as a gang-ster, as trouble. To her, he was who he could have been, whoever she made him up to be, and he knew that her version had to be better than who he really was.

"What do you think?" Amaya said, pointing to her master-piece that looked nothing like Bob's.

"It's perfect," he said, and as he watched her add her finish-ing touches, he wondered what his life would have been like if he'd had someone or something to care about the way she did.

He hadn't meant to live this way. He just seemed to be in the wrong place at the wrong time. It had been that way for as long as he could remember. In grade school he couldn't sit still or pay attention the way other kids could, and he had trouble following along—printed words and numbers were a jumbled mess. Today, he would have been diagnosed with some attention disorder, maybe even dyslexia, but back then they assumed he was slow and put him in ESL classes even though he had been speaking English his entire life. When asked to read in front of the class, he struggled, and his silence drew blank stares followed by laughter. That was the worst, a humiliation that travelled from his stomach to his cheeks in a hot rage that made him act out to avoid being acted upon. He beat up kids for looking at him the wrong way, he stole their shoes, swiped their lunches and developed both a reputation and a following. As a bully and a class clown, no one expected much from him and he stopped trying altogether. It was easier to be what they wanted him to be. He was often made to stand in the corner, sent to the principal's office and kept after class for detention. "It's not my fault," he'd say of an egged window; "What about them?" he'd ask when only his disruptive behaviour was singled out. On his report card, "Not meeting expectations. Needs Improvement," was the norm. His teachers would send notes home that he wouldn't give his parents for fear of getting into even more trouble. He was thankful they never went to meet-the-teacher nights and were too busy at work, often working graveyards or picking up extra shifts to make ends meet. Most days, Jessie and his sister came home to an empty house, ate the dhal and roti his mother had left them and watched TV. At the time, they lived with his uncle in a modest rental house on a busy road that didn't have sidewalks, but by the time he was in junior high, his dad and uncle had saved enough money to open their first pizza shop. They moved into a better neighbour-hood and for the first time Jessie felt like he fit in; he had what other people had. But this, as it turned out, only made him want more. In grade nine, when Jot bought the iconic Jordans, he wanted his own pair, and when Jot got a BMW for his sixteenth birthday, Jessie wanted one too. He hadn't realized it before, but life was like a video game; it had levels of haves and have-nots. It didn't take Jessie long to discover that if you knew the right people, you could take a shortcut or two to get everything you ever wanted.

At first, dealing in high school was just a way to make some cash to buy designer shoes, pay for gas and get a cellphone. It was easy money, and in a way it wasn't much different than working for his dad delivering pizza. The higher-ups sent him texts detailing the deliveries, and that was all he had to do—at first. When he got deeper into it, he made money off new recruits, and as he climbed the ranks, people in the community were deferential, careful to never piss him off. Although at first he liked the respect, he knew it was rooted in fear. When he was an enforcer, he took steroids, bulked up and—after a few fights that did maximum damage with minimal effort—built a name for himself. People were scared of him. Even the women that were attracted to him were just clout chasers, in it for the thrill and notoriety; they liked the idea of being in danger but were never around long enough to be in harm's way.

Devi wasn't like those girls. She knew him when he had nothing and never treated him differently when he had something. In some ways, her upbringing and conceit made her conveniently naive. She was happy to pretend that his money came from his family's pizza shops and crypto, and that her family's blueberry farm was flourishing simply because of her marketing work rather than the investment Jessie made as a favour to her brother. She didn't know that her family was on the verge of losing everything and that, had it not been for him, they would have. "It's a win-win," he'd told Jot. "A cash infusion, for the occasional use of your trucks—no questions asked." But now that their debt was paid, their grandmother wanted out of the arrangement. If anyone else had disrespected him like that, he would have sent someone to deliver a message; instead, he went to their house, had tea with the old woman and made nice. He asked after her bedridden husband, her health, and made all the necessary polite inquiries about her family before he explained the situation to her. There was no getting out. "It's nothing personal, Bibiji. It's just business."

It was for all of these reasons, and the fact that Devi was marrying Gobind's brother, Baby, that he had meant to stay away from her. After the rumours about Vegas spread, Gobind had called him and asked him to back off. They hadn't spoken since the accident. Jessie assured him that nothing had happened, which at the time was true. "Just stay away from her. You owe me," Gobind reminded him. This was also true. Had Gobind not been his stand-in that night, Jessie would have been shot. When the police came around asking questions, Gobind didn't give him up, and in all reports cast himself as an innocent bystander. Gobind wasn't known to the police and his injuries meant that his thug life was over just as it was getting started. In hindsight, Jessie figured the paralysis was a course correction, and saved Gobind from going down a road that wasn't meant for him. Gobind was smart; he had options. That's what Jessie had told him when he visited him in the hospital. He visited a couple more times, but stopped after a run-in with Gobind's dad, who told him not to show his face there again. The way Satnam Uncle had said it reminded Jessie of his own father's disappointment. Shame was what eventually kept Jessie away from Gobind, and Jessie's promise to him should have been enough to keep him away from Devi too, but then she texted him, and then she sent a nude, and then she started calling him late at night, and then last night she showed up at his place practically begging for it.

She'd walked into his penthouse and headed straight out to the deck to take in the city view, the way everyone did. Her short black dress was as tight as shrink wrap and when she leaned over the railing he could see her panties. When she came inside and sat down next to him, she tugged at the hem to keep it from riding up her thighs, a modest gesture that belied the dress.

"Some place you've got here." She stood up and walked around the room, taking in the size and scale. "Must get lonely sometimes, living on your own?"

"I keep busy," he said. "Do you want a drink?"

"Sure." She followed him, perching herself on a bar stool.

"A cosmo?" He remembered her Vegas drink.

"You know it. That was some night," she said, reminiscing about the blackjack winnings they'd gone on to lose after one too many drinks.

"Hey, did you ever find your missing friend?"

"Yeah, she was fine." She rolled her eyes. "She hooked up with some guy. But what happens in Vegas—"

"Stays in Vegas," he said, finishing her sentence as he handed her the drink.

She hopped off the bar stool and took a spin around the loft. "I love your style. It's very minimalist," she said, turning back to him.

"Is that a compliment?"

"Do you want it to be?" She smiled but he couldn't tell if she was flirting with him. She was suddenly awkward, not at all like the woman he'd been talking dirty to every night, and certainly not like the woman who asked him to say her name while he jerked off.

"So the big day? It's less than a week away," he said.

"Yep." She downed her drink and placed the glass on the coffee table.

"And you're still going through with it?"

"Of course, why wouldn't I? What's upstairs?" she said, and started up the steps.

He followed her up to his bedroom. "So why exactly are you here?"

She turned toward him. "Well, you asked to see me, remember?"

"And do you always do what you're told?" He stepped closer to her so there was no space between them, and for a moment he just stood there, his mouth hovering over hers, deciding, as if he even had a choice in the matter.

"Try me," she whispered and kissed him gently before pulling back. "Maybe we shouldn't," she said but then kissed him again, this time hard and urgent, her hands fumbling with his fly.

It was nothing like he'd imagined, nothing like they'd talked and texted about. It was clumsy at first, almost comedic in their inability to undress—his sweater snagged on her earring, her stuck zipper abandoned, dress shimmied up, his pants puddled around his ankles, shoes still on. He spun her around and bent her over, his hands on her hips, jamming his cock in with one gasp-inducing, eyes-closed push. Then the jackrabbit thrusts, the sounds of their flesh slapping, his mouth-open grunts, her crescendoed yeses, their mounting affirmations, until within minutes he shouted, "I'm coming!" and she yelled, "Not inside," and he came on her back, exhaling her name as he jerked forward. She stayed there on all fours, not moving until he handed her a towel.

"Can you?" she said, unable to reach the cum puddle that was dripping down the sides of her back. "I don't want to get any on my dress."

He nodded and wiped her down. He hated those few minutes after sex when whoever he'd just fucked was face down, or spread out—their dank sweat and sour odour cutting through the desire that made what was so necessary just moments before now violent and dirty. Devi crawled off the bed and tugged her dress down over her ass and thighs, but this time, he noted the change. It wasn't modesty, it was shame, and it was enough to make him look away. He waited for her downstairs and soon after she joined him she made up a reason to leave. He knew he wouldn't see her again, not like that. They would observe each other from a distance, at the edges of friend circles and parties, casting shadows. It's how it had to be.

That evening as he made Amaya her favourite dinner of chicken fingers and fries, he ignored Devi's ladder of texts asking him not to tell anyone about last night, asking him not to come to the wedding, asking him to stay away. He knew that what she really wanted was for him to say that he cared about her, and since he couldn't do that, since he wouldn't do that, he blocked her. In a way he was doing her a favour, because living with regrets was way better than living with what-ifs, and now at least she'd know better.

MOTTU

EVEN THOUGH SONIA HADN'T BEEN FAT SINCE OVER A YEAR AGO—AND one hundred pounds ago, the feeling had stuck. Forever the big-boned, chubby girl with the pretty face, the girl who was picked last for team sports, the girl who was friend-zoned, the girl who didn't have a bestie, whose fake friends only talked about themselves, never asking her anything about herself because—in her estimation—her fatness made her less human, less visible. Oddly enough it was that invisibility that she now missed the most. The not-being noticed was a superpower she didn't know she had until it was gone.

Now men noticed her, but which ones noticed and how they noticed seemed to be things she had no control over. Whether they catcalled in their Bostonian way or sauntered up to the bar where she worked part-time through university, they saw her as a piece of ass—their words, not hers. Then, when they got to know her, they saw her as the cool girl; she watched Sunday football, could handle her drink—for the most part—and when buzzed used the word *fuck* indiscriminately. The *fuck* thing was an old teenage habit; she figured she'd said the word so much as an attempt to hide that she'd never done the act and now that she was twenty-eight she was almost too scared to try. Sure, she'd given her share of back-seat blow jobs and let guys saddle their dicks in her ample cleavage, but she'd never gone beyond the clothes-on, lights-off bump and grind. She'd always gone home to finish herself off in the dark, pretending that she was some other version of herself. Someone smooth and plastic like Bella, her favourite porn star, who begged for harder, faster, more. Sometimes she wondered what it was like to be Bella. Did she like sex as much as it looked like she did? Did she prefer women or men? Did she have children? Was she just like the rest of us—the way celebrity magazines claimed A-listers were? For a while she was obsessed with Bella, followed her online, liking and watching, always watching.

It was Gobind and Baby who'd introduced her to Bella when she was fourteen. A bunch of neighbourhood boys had paid five dollars to watch the DVD that the brothers had found in a shoebox at the top of their dad's closet. Since Sonia's family was visiting for the summer, she'd tagged along, and unlike the boys who were loud-clowning and big-talking the whole time, she'd found herself completely absorbed, tilting her head to get a better look at the what and how of it all. The entire time she was flushed. It wasn't the prickly heat of embarrassment she was used to; this was something deep, as if someone had mixed up her insides and sent them spinning. She sat in their father's La-Z-Boy recliner with her legs crossed tightly, trying to make the pulsing stop. Scared that they could see her involuntary spasms, she did not move; wide-eyed and gulping hard, she did not speak for fear that she was about to explode.

That was the beginning of her porn habit, and even now, given the choice of what to watch and who to masturbate to, she still preferred the spray-tanned, fake-titted blondes who performed the whimpering crescendo of *oh yeahs*—a climax soundtrack that she heard in her head every time she came.

She saw Baby and Gobind only once after that summer. She and Gobind had stayed in touch for a few years, but after she started university their emails became less frequent and what was once an easy pick-up-where-you-left-off friendship was reduced to one-liners. *How are you? Fine. Busy.* She'd kept all his emails in a folder, and reread them after his accident. They'd been friends, maybe even more than that; she wrote him things that she would never have had the courage to say aloud, confessing her day-to-day insecurities, sharing the boring details of her life as if they mattered, and he always responded in kind. She could spend hours messaging him, and when they weren't corresponding she'd be saving up her commentaries as though they were only worth sharing with him. But then he got a girlfriend and his messages were shorter, always starting with *Sorry I haven't had time to message.*

After the accident, she should have called him, she should have emailed, but what was there to say that wouldn't seem like poor-you pity? Though her parents had visited Gobind's family several times since, she'd always found a reason not to go and suddenly they hadn't seemed to mind. All the hints her mother, Veero, had previously made about the two of them, their two families becoming one, abruptly stopped.

But this summer, they insisted she go with them. They, like all Indian parents with daughters of a certain age, wanted to parade her around as if this wedding was a coming-out party.

Ever since she'd lost weight, her parents had been talking her up as if she was a draft pick, listing off her stats—five foot six, 130 pounds, lawyer—to anyone who might know someone who knew someone else with whom a suitable match could be made. They weren't opposed to her having a love marriage but, having grown tired of waiting for their daughter to meet someone on her own, they were just putting it out there, or so her mother explained after Sonia had found out that she'd made her a profile on Shaadi.com, a popular matchmaking site. Veero was looking for doctors, lawyers, engineers and investment bankers, her elitism in the guise of wanting only the best for her daughter. To make her mother happy, Sonia had gone on a few coffee dates but every guy was a variation of eighties Wall Street, nineties dot-com or millennial start-up. They all wore basic tees, nice watches, expensive shoes and designer belts. They drove German cars with tinted windows. They talked about themselves a lot.

"You have to kiss a few frogs," her mother would say after every date.

"It's not the kiss they're interested in, Mom," Sonia told her, knowing that any sexual innuendo would end the conversation. "That's all these guys want." It was a partial lie that backfired; her mother then decided that American boys were the problem and cast her net wider, filtering through international prospects on Sonia's behalf. She'd already arranged for her to meet a boy in Canada during Baby's wedding week, and though Sonia was noncommittal about the meeting, Veero had never been a wait-and-see woman and had planned accordingly. Veero had been the first in her family to go to college and the first of her peers to become a doctor—which, as she often reminded Sonia, was uncommon for her time. Veero embodied the American dream, and now, since that dream included grandchildren, it meant her only daughter should marry—and soon. It wasn't until Sonia saw how many clothes her mother had bought her for the wedding that she realized the entire trip was really just a ruse to find her a husband. Yes, she would only have to meet one prospect, but surely her mother would find a way to put other young eligible men in her path.

⟨⟩

A FEW NIGHTS BEFORE THEY LEFT FOR VANCOUVER, VEERO HAULED AN oversized hard-shell suitcase into Sonia's room and hoisted it onto her bed. "You should pack," she said, opening it. The suitcase was already half-full, stuffed with sequined saris and embroidered lehengas.

"It looks like you already have," Sonia said, barely looking up from her phone.

Veero went out into the hallway and came back with a rolling rack of clothing. "I think this lehenga is perfect for the reception," she said, draping the Cinderella-like skirt across the bed.

"It's way too fancy," Sonia said, running her fingers through the layers of crinoline beneath the blue silk. "It would never even fit in my suitcase."

"We can have it shipped."

Sonia laughed but then realized her mother was serious.

"No, I'm not wearing a lehenga. The blouse is way too short."

"Stand up. Come here." Her mother ushered her in front of the mirror and held the full skirt in front of her. "You just need to get used to wearing things like this now." Sonia wondered how long her mother had pined for this mother and daughter dress-up moment. "It will look great on your new figure. Just try it on."

87

Sonia took it from her and hung it back on the rack. "Fine, I will. But later, okay?"

Veero nodded and sat next to the open suitcase. "Now, when we get there, please don't say anything about Gobind's accident."

"I would never."

"That's what you think. But it's quite shocking, you know. To see him like that. He was such a handsome, promising young man."

"Mom, I've seen people in wheelchairs before."

"Yes, and so have I, dear; but it's different when you're family. He's your cousin brother."

"Well, he's not really." The moment she said it, she knew she shouldn't have, and her mother started in about community being family and how they cherished their long-standing friendship with the Atwals.

"You're right. I'm sorry."

"It's okay," her mother said, waving it away. "But remember, don't stare."

Sonia nodded that she wouldn't. She knew what it was like to be stared at—first because of her fatness, and now because of the weight loss—and along with that came all of the stupid questions that stupid people asked: How much *did* you weigh? How much weight did you lose? What kind of diet did you go on? As if it was anyone's business. As if anything was anyone's business. She imagined it would have been even worse for Gobind. The things people would've asked.

That night before Sonia went to bed she removed the compression garments that smoothed out her layers of excess skin and tried on the lehenga her mother had chosen for her. As she'd suspected, the top was cropped beneath her bust and left little to the imagination. With fingered calipers she pulled and pinched her stomach folds and, as she tried to press her skin flat against her torso, she thought of the meat shop where they got their chicken, how the butcher pulled the skin off with his bare hands, how he cleaved the meat from the bone without getting a single drop of blood on his white apron and how he then wrapped the pieces of flesh in brown paper, asking her if that would be all. She always answered the same way. "Yes, that's everything."

THE FLIGHT TIME WITH CONNECTIONS WAS EIGHT HOURS. EIGHT hours stuck in the middle seat between her parents. Though it wasn't nearly as uncomfortable as it had been when she was heavier—her body spilling over seat boundaries, her elbows tight by her side like chicken wings—she still felt trapped. At least now she had enough room to stretch her spine, to pull the armrests down. Her father, Gurmaan, quiet on planes, sipped a Scotch before reclining his seat and closing his eyes. Sonia took a bag of trail mix from her mother and pressed the seatback screen which, unlike those of the passengers around her, did not allow her to watch any movies no matter how many times she pressed play. For the remainder of the trip she watched the flight map—the distance covered, the time remaining— while her mother drank white wine, cracked sunflower seeds and gossiped.

"It's been hard for them," her mother said, splitting a seed. "Emotionally of course, but financially too. The costs of the wedding, Gobind's care—I feel for them. I told them they should sue."

"Sue? I thought it was an accident," Sonia said.

"It was, but surely that nightclub has to take some accountability for the type of people they let in. Those people were known to the police. Had they not let those thugs inside, Gobind would still be walking."

"Did Gobi know them?"

"No, of course not. He is a good boy. Why would you ask that?" she said, looking at Sonia with disbelief. "Don't say anything like that when we get there. Don't say anything about it all."

"Okay, I won't. I was just asking is all."

Veero sighed. "It's all very sad. You know we offered to help with the wedding but your Satnam uncle is a very proud man and won't think of it. Still, it's hard to see them struggle this way. They deserve better."

"What's Baby's fiancée like?" Sonia asked, trying to lighten the mood.

Veero spat out a shell. "Rich, spoiled. That's what your auntie says."

Sonia's eyes widened. "How rich?"

"Who knows? They have a farm. Apparently Blueberry King is the biggest blueberry distributor in the country," she said in wide-eyed mockery.

"Not everyone can be a surgeon, Mom," Sonia said. "And Devi, what about her, what does she do?"

"Apparently something in business marketing," her mother said dismissively.

"Well, I'm sure she can't be that bad. Baby wouldn't marry someone who wasn't nice."

"I hope not, for your auntie and uncle's sake. They deserve some peace." She gathered the Spitz shells into a bundle and tossed them into her empty wineglass. Soon Veero fell asleep and Sonia found herself thinking fondly about her vacations out west. Though it was Gobind and Baby who had first dubbed her

Mottu, they'd never actually teased her about her weight. Mottu was just a pet name, just like Gobi and Baby, and somehow the nickname made her feel like part of the family. Sonia had grown up alone, an only child with a nanny named Anjali who lived in the guest bedroom above the garage. Anjali had taken care of her six days a week and saved her caregiving money to send home to her own children in India. She'd moved on to another family when Sonia started school and, apart from Christmas cards sent and received, Anjali had been mostly forgotten. As the cabin lights dimmed and Sonia began drifting off to sleep she wondered if Gobi and Baby had forgotten her like that too.

⸻

IT WAS PAST MIDNIGHT BY THE TIME THEY ARRIVED, AND THOUGH Satnam Uncle had offered to pick them up, Sonia's parents insisted on renting a car, and then this business of "You should have let me pick you up," and "No, no, it's fine," went on for ten minutes as they unloaded and wheeled their suitcases inside. "Just leave them there," Satnam said of the larger cases. "Baby can bring them up later. He and Gobind have gone out with friends but will be home soon."

After a few hours of conversation and cocktails her parents were asleep and snoring in the bed while she lay restlessly on a blow-up mattress on the floor, scrolling on her phone until she heard the front door open and shut. Robe on, she tiptoed out and watched from the top of the stairs as Baby stumbled over his feet and Gobind laughed. From somewhere in the house, a light turned on, and Balbir called out, "Hello? Who's there?"

Baby, finger to his mouth, shushed his brother.

91

"It's just me, Auntie," Sonia said, whisper-yelling into the darkness. "I was getting some water. Sorry to wake you."

"Okay, dear."

After a minute Sonia tiptoed down the stairs.

"Mottu?" Gobind whispered when he realized who it was.

"Yeah, it's me, but not so mottu anymore," she said, twirling and lassoing her robe's sash playfully.

"It's so good to see you." Baby hugged her full and hard in a way that she knew he wouldn't have if he'd been sober.

"That's some beard," she said, pulling away.

"Been growing it for the wedding."

"He's gotta look the part of a good Sikh boy," Gobind said. "But man, look at you!"

Sonia tightened the tie on her robe and crossed her arms over her chest, shoulders raised. "Yep. And you," she said, staring at him in his wheelchair the exact way her mother had warned against. "I mean look at you both, all grown up."

Gobind smiled and Baby grabbed her hand, twirling her around as if they were dancing. "Come on, have a drink with us," he said, pointing to the six-pack they'd brought in with them.

She sat down next to Baby, who peppered her with questions about what she had been up to these past few years. Gobind, having stared at Sonia the entire time, shook his head. "Damn, I just can't get over it, Mottu!"

"I know right? Worked out a lot. High-protein diet."

"No way."

"Way," she said, nodding.

"That's tough."

"What do you know about it?" Baby asked.

"I've seen *The Biggest Loser*. I know stuff," Gobind said.

"But she wasn't ever a loser."

"Okay guys, enough of that," she said. From working at the bar, she knew how quickly things could escalate when men were drunk.

A light in the stairwell went on. "Boys, is that you?"

Balbir climbed down a few steps. "Sonia, what's happening?" she asked, leaning over the banister.

"Nothing, Auntie," she said, hiding the beer behind her back. "I couldn't sleep and I heard them come in so I came to say hello."

Balbir nodded, lips pursed, eyebrows raised. "Well, probably best if you go to bed now, achaa?"

"Yes, of course," she said, discreetly handing the beer can to Gobind.

As she went up the stairs she heard her auntie caution the brothers on their inappropriateness. "You aren't children anymore. She's a grown woman now."

"Yeah, she is," Gobind said. Although Sonia couldn't see his face, the way he exhaled those three words made her imagine that he was thinking of her the way she had always thought of him.

THE NEXT MORNING, SONIA WOKE TO A HOUSE ANIMATED. OUTSIDE IN the driveway her father was standing like a flag person, directing a porta-potty–laden flatbed truck into a tight parking space. In the hall, Balbir was berating the decorators for having draped tulle and satin over the wheelchair lift, rendering it useless, and in the kitchen, crowded around the table was her mother, six aunties and Gobind making small talk and samosas.

"This is my daughter, Sonia," Veero announced.

"Hello, Sat Sri Akal," Sonia said, one-arm hugging each woman as they were introduced. She could not begin to remember who the aunties were and whose small children were glued to the nearby TV and which California cousins—triplets no less—were which. Without caffeine it was a blur, and growing up as a single child had not prepared her for the onslaught of distant relations.

"Chai?" she asked.

"On the stove," her mother said.

"Come sit," one of the aunties said, tapping the empty chair next to Gobind who was busy scooping the potato mixture into a dough cone. She could tell by the way they all looked at her, eyeing her up and down without discretion, that her mother had already enlisted their matchmaking skills.

"You've been promoted," Sonia whispered to Gobind, recalling that as children they were never permitted to fill the samosas and were only ever assigned the benign task of pressing their forks into the sealed dough.

"But not you." He handed her a fork.

"Where's Baby this morning?"

Gobind laughed and one of the kids turned from the screen and made a barfing face. "He's a bit hungover this morning."

Balbir shook her head. "Gobind, you have to talk some sense into your brother. Set an example. You know I don't like all this going out and drinking. Loki ki kain gey?"

Gobind raised his hands in surrender. "Hey, what can I say? He doesn't listen to me. And besides, who cares what people think?"

"I care." She smacked the side of his head. "You are his older brother, he should listen."

"Maybe he'll listen to Sonia. Why don't you come out with us tonight? You can keep us both in check," he said, never lifting his gaze from his task.

"What's tonight?" she asked.

"Just a get-together. Some of Baby's friends and some of Devi's. We thought we'd grab a few drinks at the pub before things around here go ape. What do you say?"

"Sure, sounds good. I'll just have to check with my parents first."

"Even the cousins are going," he said, motioning to the not-yet-twenty-year-old triplets whose names Sonia could not remember.

THE CALIFORNIA COUSINS—RAJ, RANJ AND RUPA—COULD NOT HANDLE their alcohol, and for most of the evening Sonia found herself acting like a chaperone, constantly wrangling them, interrupting their conversations with strange men and herding them back to the table where she could keep an eye on them. She was seated next to Devi and her two best friends, Monika and Yazmin, who were taking selfies and sipping vodka sevens.

Suddenly Devi linked her arm in Sonia's and squeezed her close as if she'd only now noticed her. "Finally! I've been wanting to talk to you all night," she said, snuggling in as if they were long-lost friends. "So Baby tells me you're from Boston."

"Yeah, born and raised."

"And?" Devi said expectantly.

"And what?"

"So do you have a boyfriend in Boston?"

Sonia turned, wriggling out of Devi's hook. "Me? No."

95

Devi winked at Baby. "So you're single!" she shouted.

"Sorry?"

"Oh it's nothing. It's just that Baby mentioned that you and Gobi used to have a thing is all."

Sonia laughed. "No, not a thing. We were just friends." Sonia glanced across the bar where Gobind was watching hockey on the big screen. "You must be so excited about the wedding," she said, redirecting Devi. "Tell me everything."

Sonia pretended to be interested as Devi told her about some end-of-the-world bridesmaid debacle involving a friend's distant cousin who stole her reception theme. "Can you believe it? The nerve, right?" Sonia, still nodding politely, zoned out, her thoughts drifting as she focused in on various parts of Devi's face. She could see why Baby had fallen for her. She was runway-model beautiful—tall and thin, no hips, small breasts, all bones and angles—her body was the perfect clothes hanger, and judging by what she and her size-zero friends were wearing, they knew it. They were overdressed for the modest pub, their bodycon dresses and contoured, smoky-eyed faces completely out of place; later, when Devi suggested they take the party elsewhere, Sonia wasn't surprised. Girls like Devi left nothing to chance. "I hear that new club on Granville is amazing."

Baby and Gobind exchanged a look.

"Not so sure that's a good idea. It's pretty hard for Gobi to navigate," Baby said.

"Oh. You don't mind, Gobi, do you?" she said, rubbing his shoulder. "We could get you a taxi home."

"Yeah, no. You go," Gobind said. "I'm good."

Baby shook his head and told Devi no.

"But it's our last night," she said, whining like a spoiled child. "Gobi doesn't mind, so why should you?"

Before Baby could answer, Sonia stepped in. "Why don't you guys go, and I'll hang back with Gobi."

Devi squealed and half hugged her, whispering that she was a lifesaver.

"You sure?" Baby asked.

"Totally."

After the squad said their long and loud goodbyes, Sonia ordered a beer.

"You didn't have to stay on my account," Gobind said, staring at the sports news playing on the TV.

"Oh, please. You're the one doing me a favour. I couldn't take another minute of wedding talk."

"She's a bit much, huh?"

"She's definitely not who I pictured Baby with."

Gobind nodded. "What can I say? My brother's pussy-whipped."

Sonia laughed. "Do people still say that?"

"Hey man, it is what it is. I mean, don't get me wrong. I'm happy for him."

"Of course you are. Still, it must be weird seeing him get married."

"I think it'll hit me when he's gone. After the wedding, they're moving back east for his residency."

Sonia took a sip of her beer. "That'll be tough. You guys have always been so tight."

"Like this," he said, crossing his fingers. "But it could be good, you know, for him to get away and start his life on his own."

She smiled, recognizing the manner in which he framed his resignation, convincing himself that everything was for the best the same way she did. "So what about you?" she asked, imitating the way their well-meaning parents spoke.

97

"I'll probably help out with the new business."

"Congrats on that," she said, toasting the air. "Frozen sweets. My parents told me about it. That's huge."

"For sure," he said, peeling the label off his beer bottle, pushing all the bits into a pile.

"What about school? Are you going to go back?"

"Sounds like you've been talking to my parents."

"Nope, not at all. I just remember how much you loved it."

"I don't know. I'm not sure anymore. I used to be the man with the plan and now I'm just—I don't know." He shook his head, avoided eye contact.

"Does anyone? I mean, sure, we all think we know what we want, but you never really know until you try."

"And what is it that you think you want?"

The way he asked made it feel like a test, and she was suddenly aware that she was good at giving the advice she could never apply. "I don't know, but as I get older I feel this immense pressure, like every decision I make is do-or-die, and now on top of that my parents want me to get married . . . They actually have me meeting some guy the day after tomorrow . . . So there's that, too." She took a long swig, knocking back the last of her beer as if it were an act of rebellion.

"So this guy, what's his deal?"

"His name is Rishee," she said, and pulled out her phone to show Gobind his online profile.

"Six foot two, engineer, loves the outdoors, enjoys photography," Gobind said, reading the bio. He flipped through the photos, his face cracking. "Sonia, I know this guy."

"You do?"

"Yeah, he's not an engineer, he's a fuckin' wedding photographer!"

"No way."

"Yeah, for real. Devi and Baby hired him."

"Serious?"

"Yeah," he said, laughing. "You still gonna go?"

"I don't know, probably."

"Well then, I'll be your out." He added her number into his phone. "I'll call you thirty minutes into your lunch with an *emergency*," he said, using air quotes. "If the date is bad, you've got a reason to leave."

"Thanks," she said, sliding her phone back into her pocket. "How about you—you must be feeling the marriage pressure too."

"Hardly," he said, gesturing to his wheelchair.

"So? What does that have to do with anything?"

"Uh, everything . . . Tell me, who's going to marry me besides some girl from India who wants to get her PR?"

"Don't sell yourself so short. Plenty of girls would marry you."

"You think so?"

"Yeah."

"Would you?"

"What? Marry you?"

"We both know it's what our parents always dreamed of." He held her hand as if he were actually proposing. "Would you marry me?"

She looked him straight in the eye and hesitated, frightened to admit that yes, she would. He was exactly the type of guy she wanted to marry. Someone who made her laugh, someone who made her feel at ease.

He dropped her hand and laughed. "See, told you so."

"Not fair. You didn't let me answer," she said, smacking his hand. "Besides, it's not like *you* would marry *me*, the OG Mottu."

"Now you'll never know," he said. "Besides, you probably have a boyfriend at home, right? Someone Mom and Dad don't know about?"

"Um, actually no. No, I don't."

"I just figured now that you're . . ."

"What? Now that I'm not fat? It's okay, you can say it."

"No, I was going to say . . . grown. Now that you're grown up."

"Right, sure you were."

"Yeah—and that you look good," he said, glancing up and then away. "I just assumed there was someone."

"Sadly, no. I mean, I've gone on some blind dates. I even tried Tinder and all that, but it's just such a hookup culture and I didn't want my first to be like that."

"Your first?"

"Oh shit. I just said that didn't I?" Embarrassed, she covered her face with her hands. "Oh fuck me—no, don't fuck me, that's not what I meant to say." Horrified, she put her head down on the table and raised two fingers. "Two vodka shots please, and quick," she said to the waitress.

"You okay?" Gobind was smirking.

She pressed her palms against her cheeks, trying to stop the flush that had crept over her face. "Please stop looking at me like that."

"Like what?"

"Like that. Like you think this is funny." She downed both shots as soon as they were set on the table. Throat burned, head cleared, she exhaled and asked for another. "It's not that I haven't done stuff, I just haven't done *it*?"

"Right." Gobind nodded, hands up. "You don't have to explain, it's none of my business."

But for Sonia the night's drink had fully set in and she went confessional, telling him how she'd always been too insecure about her body to go there. "I came close with someone once, but I backed out at the last minute. It didn't feel right," she said, omitting the part that the *someone* was a sex worker she'd hired on her twenty-sixth birthday. Naked and erect, he'd stood at the foot of the bed reminding her what sex acts were included in his rate. Cunnilingus was extra, he'd said as he climbed on top of her. He said it all so casually that it made her self-conscious and she started to laugh. Instead of having sex, they lay on the bed, stared at the ceiling and talked. She'd expected that he'd have some sad backstory that led him to this line of work, but he didn't. He was from a loving home, his parents had been happily married for thirty years, he was a grad student and this was good money. When she asked him if he ever felt ashamed, he said the idea of having sex for money didn't bother him, he was just serving a basic human need. When he kissed her neck and asked her what she needed, she didn't know how to answer and asked him to leave.

Gobind looked sympathetic. "If it's not right, it's not right."

"Yeah, he was great . . . just not for me, you know."

"I get that," Gobind said. "You can't fake your feelings. You know, I'd actually been seeing someone for three years."

"I remember," she said, thinking back to the end of their correspondence. How jilted she had felt, even though she'd had no right to feel that way.

"But after the accident, we broke up. Guess she couldn't handle it."

"I'm sorry."

"Nah, it's okay. She and I, we had planned a different life before." He stopped and signalled to the waitress for another beer. "I didn't have a choice in the matter, but she did. She got married last year."

"Ugh." Sonia stabbed her heart with her fist.

"I don't blame her. A lot of people that I used to know just fell out of my life after."

Sonia reached out her hand. "I'm sorry I never called. I don't know why I didn't. I wanted to, but . . ."

"Look, we hadn't seen each other for a long time. We lost touch. Don't worry about it," he said, raising his bottle.

They stayed there in the dim corner of the bar talking about their lives until last call. When they were back at the house, before she went up to her room, she asked if he needed anything. Though it was dark, she could see that he was considering it, and just as he said, "Yes," just as she moved toward him, he turned away and told her good night.

———◦◦———

THE FOLLOWING DAY, WHEN SONIA RETURNED FROM RUNNING HER wedding errands, the aunties were gathered around the kitchen island chopping carrots, peeling potatoes, dicing onions and singing village songs, each verse eclipsed by their laughter. Although she didn't understand most of what was being sung, she gathered—by their gestures and embarrassed faces—the songs were vulgar. She couldn't imagine these aunties in that way, making crude wedding-night jokes, talking about a man's staying power, yet there it was—sex.

Veero shushed the women when she saw Sonia standing in the doorway. "So, have you decided what to wear on your date tomorrow?"

"It's not a date." Sonia grabbed a carrot from the pile and took a bite. "It's just lunch."

"Yeah, and if you're lucky you may even get some free head-shots out of it," Gobind said, his smile cracking into laughter.

"What's so funny?" Veero asked.

"Auntie, Rishee is Rish . . . Baby's wedding photographer!" Gobind told her.

"No, the profile says he's an engineer," Veero said.

"He dropped out of school. Never got his degree," Gobind explained.

"What? Unbelievable—did he think people wouldn't find out? Lying like that."

"Who's lying?" Baby asked, walking into the kitchen.

"Auntie set Sonia up with the wedding photographer," Gobind said, filling him in.

"Oh cool. You could do worse. Rish is a good guy. Bit of a player though. Is there tea?"

"On the stove," Veero said. "And no, he's not a good guy, lying to my poor Sonia like that."

"Poor Sonia," the brothers mocked.

Flabbergasted, Veero shook her head. "We should cancel the date at once."

"It's not a date and it's fine. You heard Baby. He says Rish is a good guy, no harm in meeting him," Sonia said, revelling in the momentary I-told-you-so of it all.

"Not to worry Sonia. There are plenty of boys to choose from. Weddings are the best time to find a husband," an auntie said.

"Oh, enough now. Leave the girl alone." Balbir handed Sonia an apron and directed her to the pile of dishes in need of washing. Through the window Sonia could see the California cousins practising their bhangra routine for the reception. She watched, mesmerized, as they, former high school state champions, jumped about, banging their long bamboo sticks on the ground in synchronized patterns. Children—to whom they belonged, she was still not certain—were blowing bubbles and chasing them as they floated out of reach, and her father and uncle—sandal-footed and balanced on branches—were stringing lights through the trees.

As the day wore on, she collected these vignettes, these familial scenes, and stored them like dioramas in her mind; although she was still not used to the comings and goings of so many people, she found the assumed connection comforting.

After dinner the entire family gathered on the deck, and under the glow of the fairy lights and patio lanterns the adults sang songs just as they did when they were new in the country and had little else with which to entertain themselves. Satnam Uncle played the harmonium and Balbir Auntie and her parents sang old Hindi love songs. Sonia, unfamiliar with the words, clapped along and danced barefoot on the grass with the California cousins, who, upon an auntie's insistence, tried to teach her and Baby their Bollywood-inspired choreography.

Under the stars, their parents' songs turned melancholic. The sweet timbre of longing for other places called home pierced through her, and as she sat next to Gobind, her hand brushing his, she closed her eyes and took it all in.

Later that evening when the house fell into darkness and melodies still lingered in her head, she thought of Gobind, and texted him to see if he was still awake.

JUST THE BEST OF US

RISH WAS LATE FOR HIS LUNCH WITH SONIA, AND AS HE CIRCLED THE same downtown city block for the third time looking for a parking spot, he thought about ghosting her—but he knew that if he did, he'd never hear the end of it from his mother. She still told everyone he was an engineer and that photography was just a hobby, something he did for fun. For her, it was easier to lie, even in the online profiles, than it was to explain that he'd dropped out of university and had kept their tuition money. He didn't know what he was supposed to tell the girls she set him up with and usually just went along with the lie. It seemed only fair, given that his mother had only just forgiven him—and by forgiven, he meant that she'd stopped delivering the disappointed soliloquy that started with What did I do to deserve this? and ended with something along the lines of You should have just killed me. You should have thrown me in the well or shot me in the street like a wild dog. There were so many violent ways for Indian mothers to express their martyrdom that he heard a soundtrack of thunder and violins—like the ones in Hindi films—every time she started in on him. Haven't I done enough? What more could I have done? Why are you punishing me? He was never sure if she was asking him or God. Her pleading hands were always clasped tight as if she was holding all of her wishes and hopes inside them, believing that if she pressed them hard enough some diamond might emerge from her misfortune.

Ultimately, she blamed karma, her present circumstance a punishment for some past-life misdeed. He didn't know how to answer her with anything but Ma, please. He hated her suffering and he hated that she didn't seem to mind his. It should have been obvious that he was different. She should have noticed. He wasn't like his older, married brother who was living in New York and working at a hedge fund, or his goody-goody younger sister who was at the top of her class. The Honour-Roll Student On Board bumper sticker on their minivan had never been about him. He had been an average student and paid a mathlete to do his calculus homework. A drama kid and artist, he'd floated through high school mostly unnoticed, with the exception of that one art teacher who, in his senior year, told his parents that she thought he should apply to Emily Carr University of Art and Design. "He has real potential," she'd told them. But in their view, an education was a path to a steady job, and if you were lucky, a pension. "Stop wasting your time on these pictures," Rish's father told him. "Be sensible."

After two years of failing grades he was put on academic probation and spent the tuition money his parents had sent him on art supplies, drugs and girls. He dabbled in various forms of visual art, from portraiture to filmmaking, and even sold a few pieces at a pop-up gallery for young artists. There he met Jennie, with the long red hair and constellation of freckles across the bridge of her nose. She was covering the event for the student newspaper. Her hair was tied up, but ringlets had come loose, and when she took his picture he resisted the urge to tug at a curl just to feel the tension. Later he found her at the service exit, where some people were smoking and others huddling in the cold. Unlike those with vape pens and clouded exhales, she smoked slowly, her hand drifting as she talked. The lit end of her cigarette was the same colour as her hair. Next to them, someone was talking about a party nearby. "We should go," she told him.

Rish didn't know anyone at the party and neither did she, but since she had a camera, everyone asked her to take their photo—and even when they didn't, she wandered around inserting herself into private conversations one flash at a time. "Candid ones are the best," she said and adjusted the camera, aiming at a downward angle toward the small couch where a couple was making out on a pile of coats. Next to the couple was a girl on her phone, her bored face illuminated by the screen's glow, and by her feet was a group of people sitting and laughing around a coffee table littered with shot glasses and red Solo cups. "That's the one," she said.

At the end of the night, it was just the two of them standing in the dark alley, the street light flickering, enveloping them in a slow strobe of light and shadow, his hand on the back of her neck, his body pressing into hers, an urgency that he'd later come to understand was never about her at all. They shared a moment, a cab, a bed, all without saying a word. She taught him about analog photography and he taught her about filmmaking, and when he wasn't busy, he tagged along on her shoots. Had it not been for some random auntie who knew his mother and was at one of the weddings Jennie was shooting, his parents would never have found out—or at least not until he had a plan. He'd always intended to tell them that he was pursuing his art, but hadn't sorted out the details; to have it all come undone because of some gossipy auntie who took pleasure in outing him was the worst-case scenario.

His parents summoned him. His siblings FaceTimed him, siding with his parents in a full-on blame-and-shame intervention, telling him on repeat to do the right thing. He'd been trying to do the right thing ever since, but despite his professional success, it still wasn't quite enough for his parents; it wasn't the career they had wanted for him. Whenever he could say yes to them, he did, which is why he found himself haphazardly parking in a sketchy lot and rushing in to meet Sonia at a hot new Mexican spot.

"I'm so sorry, I had a shoot and traffic was nuts," he said, slinging his jacket over the back of the chair.

"Indian standard time, right?" Unbothered, she nodded and ordered another sangria. "I started without you," she said, munching on a tortilla chip. She was pretty in that effortless-looking way that usually took effort—a dewy complexion, a natural flush and long silky hair—only he had a feeling that she probably looked like this every day and it made him feel self-conscious. He ran his hands through his shoulder-length hair, trying to pull himself together.

"So, you're a photographer," she said.

"Yes, not an engineer. Sorry to disappoint," he said, going on the offensive before it came up. "I guess my mom left that part out of my bio."

"Classic mom move. I can only imagine what mine left out of my profile," Sonia said with a half smile that put Rish at ease.

"Probably all the interesting stuff," he said, unable to resist the urge to flirt.

"So what type of shoot was it that made you late for this very *important* date?" Sonia asked sarcastically.

"It was test shots. I've booked this wedding and the bride's family is kind of a big deal around here, so I had to get it right."

"The Blueberry King family, right?"

"You know them?"

"I'm actually in town for the wedding. Groom's side."

"Small world."

"It always is with Indian people. So, spill the chai. What are the Dosanjhs like?"

"They're alright. Pretty particular about how they want things. But for me, that's not a bad thing. I've shot weddings where people were expecting more posed portrait shots and were disappointed by my in-the-moment aesthetic."

"Hold up. I've met Devi and she doesn't strike me as an in-the-moment type of person."

"She is as long as the moment is the one she wants captured. She has a list of people she wants in the shots and ones she doesn't."

"Did I make the list?" Sonia teased.

He shook his head. "I'm afraid not, but rest assured the list is just for her side of the family."

"How about Baby's list?"

"He doesn't have one. He's been pretty chill about the whole thing, with the exception of the photos of his brother. He wants the proportions to look right, with the wheelchair and everything."

"He's thoughtful that way. The whole family is."

"It's rare. Trust me. Most weddings are drama." He paused and asked the waitress what local craft beer they had on tap, settling on some obscure hoppy local brew. "Usually there's infighting about who is and isn't invited, money tension, bride and groom family feuds, cheating, long-lost loves, exes showing up—total reality TV–type stuff."

"I don't know . . . Devi seems pretty capital-*D* dramatic to me," Sonia said, leading him along, digging for dirt. He'd heard the gossip about their recent investor and even the talk of Devi's infidelity, but he wasn't about to say that to Sonia. His work required discretion; his clients trusted him to see only what they wanted him to see. "Just capture the best of us"—that's what Devi had told him when they first met. People had warned him that she was difficult and demanding, which in his line of business was normal for a bride-to-be. Devi was no different. She was entitled, spoiled and prone to upset, but Rish, having looked at her close up through a lens, saw that it was all armour. Beneath it all she was just scared, like everyone else. Nowhere was it more obvious than in today's test shots. Dressed in her bridal clothes, she was quiet and reserved, accepting his instructions, allowing him to position her like a doll. Throughout it all she had the look of a runaway, and Rish kept his lens trained on her, waiting for the moment that she tore off her chunni and made a break for it. He imagined capturing her in mid-air, leaping out the door and across the blueberry fields, but of course that never happened; he took the photos of a woman transforming instead. She was beautiful, and not just in the way all women are in their bridal clothes. There was a vulnerability in her smile that he had not seen when they'd initially met. In the engagement photos and matrimony editorial, she'd been gleeful, almost ambitious, but now this fear, this uneasiness in the corner of her mouth made her honest, and to him, wholly good. "Just the best of us," he repeated to himself as he'd snapped shots. It seemed so simple, yet what everyone wanted was something better than themselves. "How do you know the Atwals?" he said to Sonia, changing the subject.

"My parents have known them since . . . well, forever, and now that Baby is getting married, they got the idea that I should get married, and . . . here we are."

"Ah, so you don't want to get married."

"Not like this. No offence."

"None taken."

"I'd just rather fall in love."

"Well then, cheers to you finding love," he said, raising his glass.

"And you," she said, laughing, as her phone rang.

"Is that the emergency get-out-of-lunch call?" he asked, aware that his friend would be calling him within half an hour to parachute him out if need be.

"Guilty," she said, dismissing the call.

"Wow, and you're not taking it. Does that mean we're on a date, like, officially?"

"It's just lunch, right?" she said, and put her phone away. "And at least our parents will be happy."

"And that's what counts, isn't it?" he said, recalling the arguments he'd had with them when he returned home after dropping out. Rather than tell people he didn't finish school, they told everyone he was taking a break and had come home to help his father run the family business. He didn't last a month on the job site. Even his father saw that he wasn't meant for hard labour. He didn't have the sinewy muscles, the barrel chest, the resilience of a man in need. After a few months back at home, his parents agreed to let him pursue photography. "One year, and if it doesn't work out, you finish your degree," his mother said, emphasizing the edict with her index finger. That was the deal.

"Did you always love photography?"

"Yes, and filmmaking. I like capturing what most people miss," he said, explaining that most of what he saw was not what it seemed, but what *was* real was the desire everyone had to make it memorable, to make their event show them who they were or who they aspired to be. "It's my job to find that small moment amid the chaos of their big day and serve it back to them. I make memories. That's my tag line," he said panning the air with his hands. "Years in the future when my clients are reminiscing and looking at their photos they can see who they were before they became someone else."

"I've never thought about it that way. That's intense, and kind of beautiful." She leaned forward. "You are very surprising Rish."

"Not what you expected?"

"Not at all."

The way she smiled and tilted her head when she said his name, that spark of recognition, made him wonder if she was into him or if she was just being friendly. He often found it hard to tell the difference, and he wondered if that was why he ended up dating Twinkle and why he'd hooked up with Priya before that. Had he confused kindness with genuine interest?

WHEN RISH GOT HOME, HE COULDN'T STOP THINKING ABOUT SONIA and wondered what his mother had posted in his online profile.

> I am a fun-loving and family-oriented person
> who values tradition and modernity in equal
> measure. Being passionate about technology
> and design, I studied engineering and now

JUST THE BEST OF USrun a successful construction company. In my
free time I enjoy photography, playing sports
and watching movies. In a partner, I am looking for someone who shares my morals and
family values, is career oriented and health
conscious and has a good sense of humour.

His mother had cast such a wide net that he had hundreds
of matches and he scrolled through them, passing on each and
every one of them, until he got to Twinkle. He wasn't surprised
she'd met his mother's criteria; she was perfect, everything a
mother could want in a daughter-in-law. But a few weeks ago,
when she was nattering at him about some auntie's cousin's suitable daughter, he mentioned that he'd met a girl from abroad
who was studying political science and working part-time at
Goldie's Palace. She balked at the idea. He would not be dating
an international student named Twinkle who toiled in a banquet
hall kitchen. Loki ki kain gey? was a rhetorical question. As far
as she was concerned, Twinkle's type was not good enough for
him, but Sonia was—and after having met her, Rish could see
why. She was funny and smart, independent in just the right
way. She didn't seem to want or need anything.

He scrolled to Sonia's profile.

> Born and raised in Boston, I'm a lawyer who
> loves reading, cooking and travelling. I have
> a great sense of humour and enjoy spend-
> ing time with family. I am looking for a
> professionally minded partner who enjoys
> my interests and has a mutual respect for
> Indian culture.

The profile Sonia's mother wrote did not do her justice and he sent her a text saying as much, to which she replied with a laughing emoji. He took the immediacy of her response as a sign and asked her if she wanted to go out again. He saw the three dots cycling and waited for her reply, but none came. She left him on read.

Rish's mother was disappointed, the kind of resignation that is quiet and unyielding, signalled only in the clattering of dishes, the purposeful slamming of cabinets.

"What do you want me to do about it? You wanted me to go, and I did. I can't make her interested in me."

"Yes, you can. That is exactly what you can do. You could at least try."

"I have tried. But Mom, you know I don't want to get married yet."

"Want," she said it like a swear word. "What about what I want, what your father wants?"

"Look, it's just that right now, I'm focused on my work, on building up my business."

"Business? You call taking pictures a business? No, what your father does is a business, what you do is a hobby," she said. "Even then, you'd think that taking these wedding pictures would make you want to get married. Surely at these parties there must be some suitable girls that you could choose from."

He nodded. She was right, there were lots of girls to choose from. The DJ went home with a different one each night.

"I just want you to be happy. I want you to settle down and be happy. Isn't that all we want for him?" she asked, inviting her husband, who had just walked in the door, to comment.

"Leave him be," he said, walking through the kitchen to the living room. He turned the television on and flopped into his chair. "Chai," he called out.

Rish watched his mother prepare his father's tea and place it in front of him just as she had always done. When she started to say something to her husband, his response was to turn up the television volume.

This is us, Rish thought as he watched the moment unfold and stretch over them.

HOW I WONDER WHO YOU ARE

"**S**ORRY, SORRY," TWINKLE SAID AS SHE PUSHED OPEN THE SWINGING doors of the kitchen. "The bus was late."

"Second time this week," Raju said.

"I know. It won't happen again." Twinkle fastened her apron around her waist before grabbing a fresh hairnet and gloves from the cupboard. The hairnet was one of the things Twinkle hated about working in the banquet hall. She didn't mind the chopping, and despite the scar from the seven stitches on her index finger, she had—over time—learned to love the repetition of slicing and dicing. The crack of carrots and cauliflower being chopped for subzi, the sizzle of hot oil in the cast iron frying pans and the pungent aroma of cumin and coriander reminded her of home, of her grandmother and mother. She was a vegetarian back then, and now when she called home she didn't tell them that she ate meat and fish and on occasion even drank wine; they wouldn't understand how a place can change you. Working the evenings in Goldie's kitchen, speaking Punjabi and talking about the latest Bollywood movies while testing the spiciness right from the spoon was as close to home as she could get, and the fact that everyone else was also homesick somehow made things easier. Most of the kitchen and wait staff were either international students like her or newly sponsored immigrants working to make their way, pay their debts and send money back home. Ashok had been there the longest. Sixty-seven and blind in one eye, he still worked without complaint, barely speaking to anyone other than to tell them to speed up.

Although they were not allowed to wear earplugs or head-phones due to health and safety rules, she'd learned how to tune out the sound of Raju's voice as he hollered out instructions like a reality TV show chef. She didn't even mind the steam and the heat, and joked with the other girls that it was like hot yoga minus the yoga, or like getting a facial without the spa. It was only the too-tight hairnet that she hated; when removed, it left cross-hatched marks across her forehead for hours. But even that was better than the fast food jobs she'd had, where entitled customers had mocked her accent and blamed people like her for taking their jobs and ruining their country. At least here she didn't have to interact with white people and the schedule allowed for her to go to school and spend time with Rish.

A few months ago, she'd answered an ad he'd posted look-ing for a model for an *Awaaz* bridal shoot. Thin and five foot ten, Twinkle was perfect for the job, so they'd set out in a white cube van to shoot at Queen Elizabeth Park, a popular spot for photos with its abundance of flowers, fountains and trees. She'd changed clothes in the van.

"Is Twinkle your real name?" Rish had asked between frames.

She told him yes, humming the Bollywood song that had inspired her name. Her parents loved watching Hindi movies. It was what they did together every evening. In fact she couldn't remember the television ever being off during dinner. Her father worked as a supervisor in a textile factory and her mother stayed home to take care of the house—but it wasn't a real house, at least not like the one with high garden walls that her masi lived in. Twinkle's family lived on the top floor of a three-storey apartment building. They weren't poor but they weren't rich either. They only had one servant. Deepa didn't live with them the way her school friends' servants did.

People were surprised when Twinkle decided to go abroad for school, and some—who had been to the West—told her that her life would not be so easy. "No dhal and roti ready for you, no one to iron your clothes." They were right, of course. It was her first time away from home, and she hadn't expected the feeling of desperation that comes from trying to survive on your own. For a time she'd rented a basement room from a lady she called Jasvir Auntie, and that wasn't so bad because she could go up and visit with her whenever she wanted. Being around her, watching dramas and eating home-cooked food was a balm for homesickness, but now that Jasvir Auntie had sold her house, the money Twinkle made was barely enough to pay for her newly rented basement suite with mini fridge and hot plate. She didn't even have laundry access and had to take her clothes to the laundromat, and as she sat there reading a book, waiting for the dryer cycle to finish she wondered if this was what her family's servant, Deepa, did. She'd never wondered where the clothes went, merely noticed that they reappeared perfectly folded in her drawers and hung in her closet.

She reminded herself that she was glad to have the job at Goldie's rather than the precarious under-the-table jobs that her friends worked. Half the time they didn't get paid what they'd been promised.

Sometimes Rish drove her to work so she didn't have to take two buses and the SkyTrain, but lately he'd been too busy. The day before, his mother had made him go on a blind date with some girl from Boston, and when Twinkle met up with him later that night, he seemed distracted. He said that he only went out with Sonia to make his mom happy, that he wasn't going to see her again and that Twinkle had nothing to worry about. Yet worried was all she'd been, because unlike the other times he'd gone on dates, this time he kept mentioning Sonia by name.

"So whose sangeet is it tonight?" Twinkle asked, prepping her station.

Her co-worker Rani dropped the latest issue of *Awaaz* at Twinkle's station and flipped to the matrimonial pages. "Devinder Dosanjh."

Twinkle flipped through the feature spread. "Devinder and Nanak. Cute couple."

"Cute couple? You know who she is, right?"

Twinkle shook her head.

"Blueberry King, eat like royalty," Rani sang. "Her family owns it."

"I hate that song," Twinkle said, handing back the magazine. "and now it's going to be stuck in my head."

"Come on, aren't you even excited?"

"Why?" she asked, slicing into an onion. Raju hovered over her, instructing her how to cut it as if she didn't know, as if this was not what she did every evening Tuesday through Sunday.

"Big wedding, big win!" Rani rolled up the magazine and swung it like a bat.

"What's the minimum bet?"

"One hundred bucks."

"What? No way. That's too much."

"Come on, if you win, that's at least two K."

Twinkle thought about her bank balance, her mounting debt. "I can't. Rent's due."

"All the more reason. We'll split it?"

"Okay, fine."

"Yeah?"

"Well, I can't bet without details." Twinkle grabbed the magazine back. "Dated four years, graduated, moving to Toronto . . ." she mumbled, gleaning factoids from the puff piece. "Any gossip—exes, drugs, in-law drama?"

"Check, check and check! All of the above. I heard she hooked up with her brother's friend—who just happens to be Jessie Bhatti. Apparently they were seen together at Fancy Fashions last week."

"Wait . . . *the* Jessie Bhatti?" Twinkle asked, putting the magazine down.

Rani nodded. "The one and only."

"Hmm." Twinkle considered. "She's cheating already, and with *him*?" She'd seen Jessie and his entourage at parties, loitering at the bar and getting into drunken brawls. Some said he'd been involved in a stabbing that happened in the Goldie's parking lot after a reception last month. "I bet they won't even make it to a year. I say seven months."

"Really? But look how cute they are together!" Rani pointed out their graduation photo—their heads thrown back, caps in the air. "They look so happy."

"When have I been wrong?" Twinkle said, wondering why she could call everyone else's relationships and never her own.

Rani jotted down the bet in her pocket-sized notebook. "Who else? Twinkle's down for seven months, anyone else?" she said and made her rounds, collecting bets and buy-ins. At first, the betting had just been a harmless way to pass the time and make some money, but over time, betting on their divorce rates, pregnancies—anything they could think of—had reduced the couples and their families to ratios and odds, making it easier to be in the kitchen—because really, who was serving whom? At the end of the night, the staff would settle up on the smaller bets— How many drunk uncles? How many fist fights or cat fights? How many crying drama queens? They'd sit around eating the leftovers and drinking from a few bottles they'd swiped from the bar, laughing at the host family's expense.

"It's your turn to check traps," Raju said to Twinkle.

"No way, I did it last week and the week before."

"That's what you get for being late." Raju shrugged. "Look, I'm just the messenger. Goldie calls the shots."

Twinkle took off her apron and hairnet and marched into Goldie's office, where he—middle-aged, thick waisted, wearing too much cologne—sat in an overstuffed leather swivel chair in front of his computer.

"I did the traps last week."

He was on the phone and raised his hand for her to wait. She sat across from him, taking in the cheapness of the room, the end-of-the-roll laminate, dust-covered aluminum blinds and dark-green walls with an eighties floral border that his second wife had stencilled.

"What is it?" he said when he'd ended his call.

"I did the traps last week; it's not my turn."

"It's your turn if I say it's your turn," he said without looking up from his computer screen.

"Is this because of last week?" she asked, cringing at the thought of his advances. He'd been drunk, and in truth, he was almost always drunk. A high-functioning alcoholic who dabbled in cocaine and any other substance that made him forget his age. He was always with a woman half his age and had already been married and divorced three times.

"I don't know what you're talking about. The traps, please, and quick, before the decorators arrive." He turned back to the computer screen.

Two years ago, Goldie's competitor was shut down by the health board. Not wanting to meet the same fate or draw attention to his establishment by hiring pest control, Goldie invested in traps and poisons. Before anyone arrived at the hall for an event, the traps were emptied and removed.

How disgusted Twinkle's parents would be if they could see their daughter putting dead rats into a bucket, throwing their mangled carcasses into the garbage bins and hosing down the traps, all for a minimum hourly wage. Even though there were traps everywhere there were always a few clever rats scurrying through the kitchen. The rats didn't bother Twinkle the way they did the other girls. Because of where she was from, she was used to seeing them scamper down a lane or dart from room to room. "In Rajasthan, there's a temple devoted to their worship. Twenty-five thousand rats there, and no traps! Live rats, no problem," Raju had once told them. It wasn't the live ones that bothered Twinkle, it was the dead ones, with their little heads cleaved and dangling, their little claws in the air, their little torsos squashed by the trap's spring and snap. As always, she tried not to think of what she was doing; she simply donned the industrial yellow rubber gloves and an N95 mask, and filled her bucket with dead things.

It was when she was hosing down the bucket by the service door that she saw Rish in the parking lot talking to Priya, the reporter from *Awaaz*. She called out to him but he didn't hear her. Twinkle watched the way they spoke, faces open, expressive and familiar, and she wondered if they were together. It made sense. She knew his mother was pressuring him to marry and they were well suited to each other; they'd grown up here, had the same background and probably laughed at the same jokes— all the ones she never understood, all the ones that Rish would end by saying "Never mind, I guess you had to be there." Having worked engagement parties, sangeets and receptions she could tell which couples would last by the way they looked at each other, and these two had that look—an easiness that Twinkle did not have with Rish. Their relationship had been an arrangement. He took photos of Twinkle for his portfolio, photos that she in turn could post to her social profiles and garner attention and affiliates who believed that she was someone other than who she actually was. Online, she had influence. What she hadn't anticipated were the messages from strange men asking for special pictures.

"There's a market for everything," Rish said, telling her about a website where she could monetize their demands. "You'd make a killing."

"No thanks, it's practically pornography," she told him when he'd suggested it, though later without his knowing she'd set up an account and scrolled through the options, deciding what she would be willing to do for a few extra dollars. She was surprised by how much men were willing to pay to see her naked, and it made her wonder if Rish paid someone too. Were all men like that? How foolish she'd been to call him her boyfriend. He'd never said "I love you" back. Any affection she'd thought he felt for her was only imagined. Rani had warned her that the Indians here were more casual, but she hadn't understood.

Because they were short-staffed that night, Twinkle was sent out to clear the tables. As she walked through the tight maze, picking up the half-eaten plates of tandoori chicken and papri chaat, she avoided Rish. She was glad when someone turned down the lights and she didn't have to pretend not to see him flirting with Priya. Feigning illness, she left early, and didn't even stay for Devi's entrance or the jaggo. The colourful dances, the brightly coloured potted candles balanced on top of women's heads, and the jaggo song, meant to wake up an entire village the night before a wedding, was normally her favourite part of every sangeet party—but tonight it felt like a mockery, a reminder that here in Canada she had no village, no people, no prospects.

Twinkle stole a bottle of wine from the bar and took the bus home. Unlike the first generation of mega-houses with their pink stucco and red tiled roofs, the Malhotra house where she lived was angular and modern, with a wood and stone exterior, large windows and glass railings. Nestled on a tree-lined cul-de-sac, it felt safe—the type of house you looked out of and not into. The Malhotras, who had three children under five, were a young professional couple who embodied the South Asian dream of making all their parents' sacrifices worthwhile. Whenever they were out of town—which was often, because young Indian people with money were often bored and in need of diversion— Twinkle got a small break on her rent in exchange for picking up mail, watering plants and making sure the house looked lived-in. A few weeks ago she'd seen the invitation for the Dosanjh wedding in their mailbox and had thought about attending. So many of her classmates attended parties they weren't invited to for the free food and drinks. If anyone asked them who they were, they just lied and said that their families were from the same village. With hundreds of guests, the hosts never really noticed who was there, only who was not.

Rather than returning to her suite, with its low ceilings, subterranean window-well views and bad Wi-Fi, Twinkle watched TV on the Malhotras' big screen. When Rish called an hour later, she thought about not answering but couldn't resist.

"Hey, you left early," he said, getting right to it as he always did. She used to like that about him, mistaking his directness for ambition, confidence even.

"Yeah, I was tired and I had homework to do." She tried to sound disinterested.

"After I'm done here, I can come by," he said. "If you want."

"What? No plans with Priya or Sonia?" she said, mentally distancing herself from that night when they'd drank a bottle of champagne and pressed against each other in the back of his van. He wasn't her first but it still mattered to her.

"No, I never had any plans." He sounded confused. "Did I do something to upset you?"

She paused, listening to the hum of the party in the background. "No, I'm just busy." She was cool about it, parroting the tone he used when she called and interrupted his work. "I have to go," she said, and hung up. When he called back, she didn't answer, and instead opened the bottle of wine she'd taken from the party, taking swigs while walking down the hallway, turning the lights out. The house was spotless. Even the children's rooms seemed staged, stuffed animals propped and posed, books face-out on shelves. She'd never seen the children play outside, or even swim in their in-ground pool, and she wondered what it was all for. What was the point? It seemed like such a waste. She thought about her cash-strapped friends, who used the food bank or ate their meals at the gurdwara, who had nothing, and no better choices to make, while people like the Malhotras and Rish talked endlessly about their dreams. Imagine!

Emboldened by the wine, she went into the master bedroom closet, undressed and thumbed through Mrs. Malhotra's designer clothes, slipping in and out of her skin. She tried on the red-bottomed stilettos that cost twice as much as Twinkle's monthly rent. She thought about what Rish had said about making a killing on her photos, and undressed, taking a suggestive photo of herself in those shoes. She then took off her bra, pulled one of the designer bags from the closet shelf and sat on the chaise longue, holding the Birkin bag over her chest the way she'd seen in high fashion magazines. She cropped out her face until the image was only neck and shoulders, torso, side breast, purse, legs and shoes. In that photo she could have been anyone. She pressed post.

Afterwards she put everything back in the closet, and as she tidied up after herself, she wondered what Deepa, her family's servant in India, had done to survive. Had Deepa read her books and napped on her bed? Had she tried on her mother's saris? Did everyone play pretend? As her phone chimed and buzzed with hearts from all over the world, she realized that Deepa was lucky to never have needed an audience.

A GAGGLE,
A MISCHIEF,
A MURDER

RAMAN WAS ALREADY TIRED; IT WAS ONLY SIX THIRTY, BUT BECAUSE she'd been up at five a.m. making last-minute arrangements for the sangeet party as the mother of the bride, she was exhausted and stifling yawns. Standing at the front of the receiving line, she fiddled with her lehenga blouse, that itchy jewel-encrusted bodice that she was sure was too tight and too short for her age but that Devi had insisted would look good in the pictures. Raman had lost ten pounds just to fit into it, consuming nothing but water with lemon and cayenne pepper for two weeks. Whenever she felt hungry, she ate a breath mint, chewed gum vigorously or added a dollop of maple syrup to her water until the acidic cramps and nausea passed. This not eating was exactly the sort of thing she'd told herself she would never do. She wanted to age gracefully the way her mother had. Her fresh-faced mother, who wore plain silk saris, hair in a bun and the same gold hoop earrings every day, would never have gone on a fad diet or had Botox injected into her forehead. At Devi's behest, Raman had started the treatments a year ago, a long thin needle poked square between the eyes every few months until the small brackets between her brows were no more. People commented on the change in her appearance without being able to say exactly what had changed, only that she looked rested. Strangers now mistook her for Devi's older sister, then would remark on how good she looked for her age. She was only twenty when she was married off to Devi's father, Bhajan, and sometimes wondered if things would have been different had her mother not died in the car crash. Raman had driven right by it on her way home from school, not realizing that it was her parents. Her father had been wearing a seat belt. Her mother had not.

The year after Raman's arranged marriage, her father also remarried, splitting his time between India and Canada until his new wife gave birth to his only son. Raman was glad her father had decided to settle in India and spare her the embarrassment of having to defer to a stepmother younger than she was.

Because of Devi's wedding, Raman had been thinking about her own mother more than usual, and as she took in the banquet hall decorated with vignettes of village life and Rajasthani colour, she was sure her mother would have found the staging distasteful. There were spinning wheels, ox carts, pottery and velvet settees beneath Mughal columned archways—set props against a backdrop of bright silk swags, artificial trees with garlands of marigolds and jasmine dripping from their branches—all of it meant to provide photo opportunities for the girls lining up to pose and post. There was an elaborate row of decorated food carts where guests could order street food just as they would in New Delhi, and just beyond that was the open bar complete with a signature mango-infused cocktail, the saffron sun. Goldie's catering staff, in their peacock-blue uniforms, artfully balanced platters above their shoulders as they wove through the crowds, serving and clearing dishes with almost choreographed precision. "What shenanigans!" She could almost hear her mother's disdain. That's how it was when she thought of her mother; instead of nostalgic memories, Raman actually heard her mother's voice speaking to her from somewhere behind her shoulder, always out of sight. "Raman, stand up straight," she heard her mother say, remembering the way she'd poke her index finger between her shoulder blades to force the alignment. "Chin up, eyes down." Be proud and modest, seen not heard; know who you are speaking to. Advice her mother had bestowed on her in small chunks while chopping onions or washing dishes. Her mother had been fastidious, and only recently had Raman come to realize that her mother might have had OCD—perhaps that was the name for her mother's incessant handwashing, her hair brushed one hundred times on each side, her sari's ironed accordion pleats, her precisely executed daily cleaning that had to be done an hour before Raman's father came home from the mill. As a child, Raman didn't know what he did there, only that he came home smelling like heat and sawdust, never showering until after everyone was asleep. Even now, whenever she smelled cedar or sandalwood in a cologne it made her think of him up close and at night, his chainsaw smell, metal and sweat and wood chips, his raspy voice telling her to be a good girl. She'd never told anyone, not then and not now. "It was your fault anyway." It was her mother's callous voice that she heard—or maybe it was her own. At times it was hard to tell. Like her mother, she had become accustomed to accepting what she didn't want and it had made her bitter, like the pit inside a fruit.

As she scanned the hall she saw her distant cousins seated at the far end, relegated to the worst table—the one closest to the bathroom—just as they had been when they were younger.

She had not seen them for years and wondered if they felt some obligation to make an appearance on behalf of their dead parents. There were six of them, these sisters. Though they didn't look alike when they were young they'd been indistinguishable in their drab hand-me-downs that cycled from one to the next, hopelessly out of style by the time they reached the sixth sister, Meena.

Most people remembered them by birth order: the oldest, the youngest, the fourth or the third, all lined up for guests like the Trapp Family Singers less the song. In front of adults they had been silent, their mother listing their names, stringing them together in one long *inder-jinder-jeet* exhale for anyone who didn't know which was which. There they'd stood, their long black hair parted in the middle, slicked back in low ponytails. From behind they looked like stick figures, just limbs and hair, nothing special save for their fair skin and large eyes. Whenever Raman's mother caught her gawking at them she'd tell her to stop, for there was nothing to look at. They had nothing, these girls: no father, no money, no prospects. They had nothing. It bore repeating. But Raman knew this was not entirely true. They had each other—and at times she found herself desperate to belong to their little club. At other times she hated them for all the attention they garnered. What do you call a group of Indian girls—a pack, a gaggle, a mischief, a murder?

Over the next hour, Raman circulated through the maze of tables with her freeze-frame smile, greeting distant family members with some variation of So nice to see you, and Thank you for coming, finally making her way toward the sisters.

When the sisters were young, Raman's mother had invited them over to dinner at least once a month. "They're less fortunate, and they're your cousins," she would say, even though they weren't actually her cousins. It was their mothers who were cousins, or perhaps it was their grandmothers who were cousins; she couldn't recall exactly, and back when they were young it hadn't mattered. Everyone belonged to someone. The community was a village and everyone took care of each other. Whenever the girls visited, her mother had insisted Raman be nice and allow them to play with her toys. "This is Malibu Barbie." Raman remembered standing in front of them like a teacher, holding the doll in the air. "My father bought it for me and it wasn't even my birthday," she'd boasted. When they told her how lucky she was, she'd pretended it was nothing, like it didn't even matter, and tossed the doll in the corner with her Easy-Bake Oven, hairdressing doll, and Barbie camper van—all the coveted toys that they would never be able to afford. And even though it was them who were visiting her house and playing with her toys, she was the one who felt like an outsider, misinterpreting inside jokes and knowing laughter as personal slights. Whenever she felt that way, she'd find a way to mention her father, to remind them of what they did not have. Sometimes she'd give them a toy she no longer wanted and then at the last second change her mind. Their disappointment was a thrill.

It was only after Raman was married that she learned that it was the second oldest sister, Parm, who'd been Bhajan's first choice, but Parm had been betrothed abroad and Raman was the runner-up. It was her mother-in-law who told her this. How different things might have been had she not married him. She did not have a happy marriage, nor did she have the terrible one that her daughter insisted she'd had. Ever since Devi had taken a university course in child psychology she'd blamed trauma for all her personal failings. According to Devi, Raman was codependent. "Everything was always about Dad. You never cared about me and Jot," she'd said. And what was Raman to do about that? Apologize? Devi's recollections of events, her misremembering, had caused an unspoken rift between them. Memory was slippery, changeable, and as Raman hugged, greeted and thanked guests she wondered what she might be misremembering about those sisters.

No longer the poor relations, they were well-dressed with perfect hair and makeup, almost Kardashian-like with their dark hair and ageless skin. Meena, the youngest, a writer who had written a scandalous memoir, was even wearing a cream and copper lehenga that, from a distance, looked similar to her own. Oh, the gall! Seeing Raman approach, the sisters stood up to receive her. Raman moved around the table, hugging each of them in a one-armed embrace. "So good of you to come. It's been too long," she said to all of them at once. "And is this—?" She paused on the seventh.

"My daughter, Leena." Meena nudged her daughter forward the very way their own mother had encouraged them to say hello, to say thank you, to be polite.

The striking young woman nodded. "It's Lee." She had a bored look about her, barely making eye contact, acting the same way Meena had when she was that age. Meena had always been the rebellious one, and look at how things had turned out for her: sad, alone and awful, with no one to blame but herself.

"Congratulations," Meena said.

"I still can't believe my baby is getting married," Raman said and smiled at Lee, who had her father's blue eyes and fair skin. She almost said as much, but, feeling sorry for them, refrained. She wondered how it was for them, knowing that every time they went to a party like this, with people like her, they'd be forever shamed. If Raman were in their shoes, she probably would have moved towns to get away from the gossip and endless side-taking. She certainly wouldn't have written a book about her abusive marriage and subsequent affair. Raman wasn't sure if Meena's decision to air her dirty laundry was stupid or brave, and she'd gone to the writers' festival to hear Meena speak. During the Q&A, a man in the crowd had said that her book painted the Indian community in a poor light. Meena was calm, replying, "A book cannot represent the experience of all people, only the people within the book."

"Not all Indian men are abusive," the man stated.

"No one said they were," Meena said, looking directly at him. Raman had been enthralled, mesmerized by Meena's truth telling the same way a child might be mesmerized by an open fire, sparks be damned. She watched others stand in line to have their books signed but thought the better of it.

"How long are you in town?" Raman asked Parm.

"Just for a few more days. I'm afraid I'll miss the wedding." Parm had a British accent now, the put-on kind you get when you've been immersed. She'd lived in the UK for almost all her adult life.

Raman smiled, relieved that she wouldn't have to see Parm again. That she wouldn't be reminded about being her husband's second choice. "Well, I'm so glad you came tonight," she said, encouraging them all to try the saffron sun before heading off to socialize with other guests. But no matter who Raman spoke to, she couldn't help but look back at them, curious and envious of their togetherness, of how happy they looked. What did they have to be so happy about? They had nothing.

THE LIGHTS DIMMED AND DEVI MADE HER CHOREOGRAPHED ENTRANCE. With a dozen of her cousins and friends buzzing about her in colourful outfits, she acted the part of a shy bride. Once on stage, her friends danced around her, throwing marigold petals in the air, rushing to and from her side, pulling her in sync with their movements, hips swaying, arms in the air. The fullness of their Anarkali suits opened like flowers in their perfectly timed twirling until the music stopped and the spotlight shone on Devi. She shook her braceleted wrists in the air, lip-synching the first few bars of "Bole Chudiyan" as her friends lined up behind her and re-enacted the Bollywood choreography. They had been practising with a dance instructor from Mumbai for six months. He'd worked with all the stars, and Devi had had to cut friends who couldn't keep up with the gruelling schedule or master the intricate movements. Usually these family dance numbers were clunky, with everyone falling a step behind the beat; Raman had never seen anyone pull off a production like this. Even the choreographer had been skeptical, but Devi had assured him that she was not like other girls. And to her credit, the dance was as magnificent as any Bollywood number. When it was over, Devi, bejewelled and triumphant, took her seat in the throne-like chair centre stage while her best friend, Yazmin, introduced the next guest, Sajin Singh. She was an Instagram poet, whose books had sold millions of copies—why, Raman was not sure. The books were, in her mind, nothing more than collections of aphorisms accompanied by line drawings, but Devi was a fan and had even tattooed a half-shaded circle on the back of her neck in tribute to the poem "1:1." Raman remembered how, at nineteen, Devi had held up her hair to reveal the tattoo and then recited the poem—"1:1 is a ratio, / two halves, / make whole"—as if it meant something. With the lights now dimmed, Sajin Singh recited her lines theatrically, the accompanying illustrations projected on large screens around the hall. After each poem there was near silence, the packed hall as quiet as it could be with its hundreds of guests. Sajin Singh ended her recitation with a poem and line drawing that Devi had commissioned for the occasion. On screen, a tree with heart-shaped fruit captioned: "Love is the root, / Love is the fruit." Applause as the poem then faded into a slide show of home movies and still photos accompanied by Devi's favourite Beyoncé song, "Halo."

Raman welled up as she watched her daughter growing up on screen: birthdays, school trips, summer holidays, party hats and presents. Her only daughter was getting married and leaving home, and soon Devi's life would start anew just as Raman's had when she married Bhajan so many years ago. Is this what her mothering had amounted to? Love is the root, love is the fruit. The words rang in her ears. She had never loved Bhajan, and she suspected he felt the same. When she was a newlywed, she'd had a flirtation with a handsome farmhand with hazel eyes, and when he asked for more, she had him fired. That was as close as she'd ever been to love.

Over the years, Raman had told herself that she stayed with Bhajan because of the children, always promising herself she would leave him when they graduated high school, when they finished university, when they got married, when, when, when— but never . . . and now—she couldn't finish the thought. The idea of her daughter rooting her life in someone else's that way made her queasy. Was that all she had taught her? To attach? She wondered if Devi was even in love with Baby. She too had heard the rumours about Devi and Jessie Bhatti. It wasn't too late for Devi to change her mind, or even to know her mind. She could still call it off.

Raman, having drunk too many saffron suns, wanted to yell "Stop!" and rush to the stage and ask her daughter if a husband was what she really wanted—but how could Devi even know what she wanted? Women were raised to exist in relation to and in validation of another—a mother, a sister, a daughter, a niece, a wife—and that is all Devi was: root and fruit. The stupid poem seemed to take hold of her body and as her thoughts circled, she was sure she felt it—a sharp current, needling her calf, circling her leg. She looked down at her lap; something was rustling under her skirt, inside the crinoline. Horrified, she clamped down on her thigh until whatever it was had stopped moving. While everyone was glued to the slide show Raman hobbled to the washroom. Once she was in the stall she unclenched her hand and shook the fabric of her skirt, shrieking when she saw a rat fly out of the crinoline and into the toilet. Instinctively she flushed the toilet and leapt out of the open stall, watching in horror as the water rose, the tail circling up and up and almost over.

"Are you alright?" It was Meena, emerging from another stall.

Raman thought she had been alone. "I'm fine, it's nothing," she said, trying to close the stall door.

"Oh my god." Meena said, having seen the rat.

"It had crawled up my skirt and I—"

"Crushed it."

Raman looked down at the bloodstain on her lehenga. "Shit."

"I'll go get some help," Meena said, turning toward the door.

"No, don't." Raman grabbed her arm. "No one can know."

Meena looked confused. "But you need some help. What if it bit you?"

"It didn't. I'm fine. Besides, what will people think if they find out? It'll be all they talk about. The whole party will be ruined."

Meena nodded, and gestured toward the toilet. The water was dribbling over the bowl.

"Oh no." Raman was panicking.

"Lock the door." Meena pulled reams of paper towel from the dispenser, wrapping her right hand in a thick brown wad. With squinted eyes, she held her breath, leaned over the toilet and skimmed the water, scooped the rat into her paper glove and then tossed it in the metal garbage bin. "There," she said, as she washed her hands with hot water, scrubbing as if she were a surgeon. "No one needs to know, right?"

"Right, thank you," Raman said as she watched Meena wash up.

"Now, we should take care of that bloodstain." Meena pulled Raman toward the sink, blotting the stain with cold water until it had softened from red to pink.

"Now people will just think I spilled red wine on myself. I guess that's better than them worrying about rats running around the food carts."

"Street food. Rats. It's authentic," Meena said, trying to make light of the situation.

Raman leaned in toward the mirror and sighed. "I just wanted everything to be perfect for her."

"Of course you did. That's all anyone wants for their kids."

Raman nodded and stared at the stain.

"Let's switch," Meena said, yanking off her lehenga skirt. "They're similar. It's dark; no one will be able to tell the difference."

"I couldn't."

"Yes, you can." She was already stepping out of her A-line skirt. "Look, I was getting ready to leave anyway. No one will notice, and even if they do it's no big deal. They're always talking about me anyway; this'll just be something new for them to gossip about."

"No one talks about you."

"Come on, sure they do." Meena handed Raman the skirt and waited for her to hand hers over. "I'm still every bibi's cautionary tale. I can almost hear them saying 'Don't be like her' when I walk by."

"Well, I think you're brave, and your daughter, she's beautiful. She has his eyes."

Raman slipped on Meena's skirt. "I'm sorry I wasn't there for you."

"It's okay. It was a really long time ago. You had your own marriage to deal with. Things were different then."

Raman nodded, even though she knew things weren't any different now, at least not for her, and maybe not even for her daughter. She still did what was expected of her. She was weak and always had been. She wasn't the survivor she liked to pretend she was; she was the woman who settled for less for fear that less was better than nothing, as if those were the only options.

⸻ ❧ ⸻

THE FOLLOWING MORNING DARSHAN HAD ALREADY MADE TEA AND WAS sitting at the kitchen table sifting through a stack of envelopes when Raman came in.

"I've been waiting," her mother-in-law said. "We have to open the cards." Darshan motioned to the bounty of early wedding cards, all with undisclosed sums of money inside.

"Can we do this later?" Raman said, pressing her temple.

"You drank too much."

"No, I'm fine," she lied.

138

"I saw. Don't think I didn't see." Darshan slid a letter opener through one of the envelopes and, as she opened the card, a hundred-dollar bill fell out. "Women in my day didn't drink. They knew their place." She handed the dollar store card to Raman and asked her to read it.

"From cousin Sandeep and family," she said, wiping the glitter off her fingers and onto her housecoat.

Darshan retrieved her little black book from the kitchen drawer. "Write it down." Raman took the book from her and flipped to a blank page. Darshan had been cataloguing these gift exchanges for years; what was given would eventually be returned. "Sandeep, one hundred dollars," she said, marking it down. Darshan slit another envelope, this time retrieving five hundred dollars.

"Who's it from?" Raman asked.

Darshan, who was now wearing her readers, looked the card up and down. It was one of those expensive handmade cards, adorned with lace and pearls. She handed it to Raman. "Your cousin, Meena."

"Generous," Raman said, writing it in the book.

"Mmm," Darshan said, taking off her glasses. "I was surprised she even came."

"Well, we did invite her."

"It was an invitation out of respect to her mother." Darshan shook her head dismissively. "She should have understood that."

"Come now, it was more than twenty years ago. She was young and in love. Maybe we should just let it go?"

"She brought shame to her family. It is unforgivable."

"Well, I thought it was nice that she came."

"Nice? Pfft," Darshan said, slicing another card open as if it were a neck. "When she came to give me the card, I saw she had a big red stain on her lehenga. Wine probably. Divorced women—you know how they are. Your bhua Jasvir said she saw her at the bar a few times, lined up with the men. What kind of woman goes to the bar like that, standing with men? A divorced woman, that's what kind. They have no shame."

"I don't see the big deal. Times have changed," Raman said, remembering Meena's kindness.

"Times may change. People do not. The expectations remain. All marriages have troubles but you stay and work through them the same way I did, the same way you did. The same way Devi will. It is our culture. For your cousin to do what she did, and with a gora—there was no excuse. Shameless."

"But men cheat all the time."

"They are men," Darshan said. "It is not the same. Women don't cheat."

Raman shrugged, only half listening to her mother-in-law spin stories about a woman's place. She knew that she should have told the truth about the stain, about the rat; she should have said something more in Meena's defence, or in support of her daughter's future, but instead she said nothing and simply recorded the names and sums of what was given and what was taken, knowing it would never add up.

LOVE LANGUAGES

LIKE MOST PUNJABI FAMILIES, THE ATWALS DID NOT TALK ABOUT THEIR feelings. Baby's parents had never told him they loved him, but of course he knew that they did. Food and provisions were proxies for love and community, and for as long as he could remember his mother had asked him "Are you hungry? Have you eaten?" several times a day. When he was younger, he'd wished he had a sitcom family with life lessons and a laugh track, but as he got older he had realized that those families didn't actually exist. Most everyone was doing their best. At least that's what his friend Anne had told him. He hadn't seen her since his stag and Devi preferred it that way. Devi didn't think women and men could be just friends and lately he wondered if she was right. Nothing had ever happened between him and Anne, but it had always felt like it could have—and unlike all the boy-meets-girl stories, they did not have a love-conquers-all happy ending. In fact, he was sure that it was life that conquered all, not love—at least not romantic love, not for him. But he still held out hope that he and Devi would find their way back to each other and that all the tremors and troubles under the surface were just stress impressions from planning the wedding. He loved her as best he could. That's what he was thinking about when between pre-wedding errands he squeezed in an appointment with life coach and self-love expert, Peter. Baby's father had picked Peter up in his taxi and had referred Gobind to him, saying that he believed Peter was put in their path to help Gobind. As far as Satnam was concerned, it was fate. Baby's father had always favoured his brother, but it had become more obvious after the accident; everything revolved around what Gobind needed or wanted. Baby, not wanting to pile onto his parents' mounting stress, did what was expected, which in his case was to not cause any trouble. He didn't blame them for not paying attention to him; they probably couldn't even imagine a world where he needed help. Normally, Baby would have talked to Gobind in a roundabout way, but ever since Sonia came to town, the two of them were smitten and inseparable. He was happy for them, truly, but he could hardly count on Gobind to be objective about matters of the heart now.

According to Peter's website and TEDx talk, self-love was a prerequisite to true love. Baby had never thought of it that way. He didn't hate himself, but he wasn't in love with himself either.

"I'm just me," he told Peter when they met that morning for their in-person session. Peter got up, picked up a football that was sitting on a bookcase and tossed it in the air, catching and releasing it as he paced the length of his office. Throwing a football while talking was something Peter did on his Instagram reels and Baby wondered if he thought it made him more relatable, more dad-like. Baby half expected Peter to call him *son*. He tried to see what his dad saw in this khaki-wearing white dude who looked like he'd played college ball and golfed on the weekend.

"And what does that mean, Baby?" He tossed the ball to Baby. "What does it mean to be you?"

By the way Peter had paused before he said *you*, Baby could tell that he was supposed to have some deep answer—but he didn't. "I don't know." Baby passed the ball back.

"Sure you do. Think about it." He fake-passed in a way that made Baby flinch. "Who are you? What words would you use to describe yourself?"

"Honest, I guess."

"Okay. Continue, and no guessing."

"Kind."

Peter set the ball down and leaned against his desk, gesturing for Baby to go on.

"Good . . . I generally try to do the right thing."

"And what is the right thing?" Peter asked pointedly. "For you, right now."

"I'm not sure. That's why I'm here."

"Let me put it to you another way." He paused and crossed his arms the way a coach would before delivering some inspirational monologue. "What are you worried about?"

"I'm worried that getting married is a mistake."

"Okay, that's a great start. Why would it be a mistake?"

"Well, like I mentioned on the phone, I think my fiancée cheated on me and it's kinda got me messed up."

"And what makes you think she cheated on you?"

"Things I hear. Rumours."

"And what did she say about these rumours?"

"She didn't," he said. "I mean, I didn't really ask her."

"Why not?"

"I don't know."

"Sure you do. Don't think, just answer."

Baby paused and took a breath. He knew that if he were to ask Devi, she'd deny it, because either it was true and she'd never admit it, or it wasn't true, which would then lead her to resent him for his mistrust. There was no winning. Not for either of them. "Because there's no point."

"Right, exactly!" Peter leaned in. "There's no point because this isn't about her. It never was! You see that now, right? That it's about you? It's about what you want to do. You can't control what she does or did. Only what you do . . . So what do you want to do?"

"I want to get married. I want to get on with it . . . start my life, you know?"

Peter nodded and sat down in the chair across from Baby. "Hate to break it to you, bud, but your life started long before you ever met this girl. She's just part of it now—you need to remember that."

"Right," Baby said, trying to let that land while Peter kept talking. It was true that Devi was only part of his life, not his entire life—but his life also included his family and her family and all of their combined expectations. To Baby, it didn't seem as simple as Peter was making it out to be, and it made him wonder if white people were just built different, always elevating the individual over the community, always taking care of number one. "It's a Western thing," Anne had once told him after having written a cultural commentary. "Rugged individualism. It's the reason why their kids leave home at eighteen, why their elders live in homes. It's a me-versus-we, youth-obsessed culture. The rest of us—we take care of our own. We value selflessness over self-centredness." He'd agreed with everything she said and told her how his mother, while on a flight to India, scoffed at the flight attendant who reminded everyone that in the event of an emergency, adults were to fasten their own oxygen masks before helping a child. There was no world where his mother would not help her children first. As an Indian, you did right by others even if it was wrong for you. No one had ever said this to him, but he knew it as sure as he knew anything. You did what you could to protect the people you loved, even at your peril. It's the reason he and Anne had never dated. His parents would never have approved. They weren't racists; they were realists. It was easier to marry an Indian, to never have to explain and defend the way things were, the way he was.

Peter, seemingly satisfied with what he thought was progress, smiled. "Time's about up. We can pick this up next time."

Baby nodded and shook his hand even though he had no intention of coming back. There was nothing Peter could show Baby about himself that he didn't already know.

After Baby got in his car, he reflected on the session and how comical it was with all the football throwing. Anne would have gotten a kick out of it; it was something they would have re-enacted; it would have become an inside joke. He missed her and thought about calling, but then he thought better of it and went to see Devi instead.

WHEN BABY ARRIVED AT DEVI'S HOUSE, HER BROTHER, JOT, WAS OUT front helping unload a party rental truck full of elephant statues of various sizes. "What's good?" he said, greeting Baby.

"You know . . . Countdown is on."

"Tell me about it. Devi is in full-on freak mode. You sure you don't want to duck out? I won't tell her you were here," Jot said, laughing.

"It's all good. Where is she at?"

"Around back, supervising the patio light install for the mehndi party tonight—and by supervising, I mean yelling at everyone."

"Sounds about right."

"You want me to go get her?"

"Nah, I'll go on back," Baby said and headed toward the side gate.

"Don't say I didn't warn you," Jot yelled.

The Dosanjhs' back deck had been transformed into a Mughal courtyard, complete with handcrafted swings, cane furniture and brightly coloured bolsters and cushions. Before Baby could see Devi he could hear her shouting at the decorators about the spacing between the bronze lanterns.

"Hey, this looks amazing," he yelled over her tirade.

"What are you doing here?" she asked, rushing over. "I thought we agreed not to see each other until the big day." She grabbed his hand and pulled him along, not waiting for his reply. "Walk with me, I need to get out of here." By the way she said it, Baby thought she had something urgent to tell him, but she didn't, and as they walked out of the yard and into the fields, she prattled on about the mehndi station not having enough stools, and how her kaleeras were only two layers, not three, and that she hoped they'd look good in the pictures. "Everyone is so incompetent. I asked for peacock feathers and they brought me ostrich. Can you believe it? White ostrich." As she went on, Baby wondered if attention to detail was her love language; maybe her desire for perfection was an expression of love rather than control—or maybe it was both. Did Devi love him, or was he just there to fill some void in her life, something she could not love

146

about herself that she was trying to cover up the way Peter said people did?

"Hey, I know things have been tense these last few weeks," he said, interrupting her monologue.

"And?" She stopped mid-step and looked at him like someone who was preparing for bad news.

"And . . . I just wanted you to know that I know things'll get better. We just have to get through the next few days. And as for all the details, don't sweat it. Everything looks great."

She sighed and started walking again. "You're right, it does look great. But I am going to get the peacock feathers," she said, laughing at herself. "I do love you Baby, you know that right?"

"Of course I do," he said, aware of how good it felt to hear it.

LUCKY, LUCKY BOY

IN GOBIND'S DREAMS, HE COULD FLY. HE KNEW IT WAS A COMMON dream, a normal response to stress, a subconscious desire for freedom, but ever since the accident, it was the only recurring dream he'd had. Before, most of Gobind's dreams were the regular anxiety-driven manifestations of having one's teeth fall out, appearing suddenly naked or falling from a great height, but now it was flying. Not flying the way superheroes did—with billowing capes and Lycra costumes—but the way birds did, effortless soaring and swooping, gliding on jet streams. At times, dreaming had been the best part of his day, but lately his flight patterns had gone off course; he'd lose control and fall, his body tumbling and pinballing off clouds. He'd wake up in the dark, startled upright and sweating, a scream lodged like a fist in his throat until slowly his eyes made shapes from shadows. His chair in the corner, his legs motionless under the covers, rigid and still as if they were set apart from the rest of his body. He'd read online that being able to fly in a dream meant that the dreamer was trying to free themselves of a problem, or that the flight signified hope and new possibilities, and for him, both were true—yet he didn't feel like he had the power to deal with Jessie, or the right to take things further with Sonia.

That dream had become a reminder, a marker of what he could not have: freedom. That's what he missed most, the freedom to move, to do and go where he pleased without having to check for ramps and lifts, for widened aisles and automatic doors, for accessible transport. He tried to remind himself how lucky he was. If the bullet had hit differently he could have been like Tom from group with the c6 injury. Tom's pickup truck had rolled down an embankment on the Sea-to-Sky Highway after being hit head-on by a drunk driver. He said he saw it coming and closed his eyes, heard the crush of metal, the cracking of branches like bones, and when the car finally stopped rolling he opened his eyes. "All I could see was broken glass and the time flashing in red on the dashboard display: 12:07 a.m." He told the story over and over, each time adding in more details—it was warmer than on previous nights, the Black Keys were playing on the radio and he'd turned it up, because even though he didn't like them, he liked that one song, "Lonely Boy." At first he felt it all in slow motion, his car floating over the edge, soaring in the air before it nosedived and tumbled all the way down. It was as if, in his retelling, Tom was filling in the blanks, or trying to finish a puzzle. But no matter how he told the story, he always ended it by reminding himself and anyone who was listening how lucky he was to be alive.

Gobind was lucky too; even the doctors said so. The accident could have been so much worse. Everyone called the shooting an accident even though it wasn't, not really. That bullet was meant for Jessie; Jessie was the one who was supposed to work the club that night. Jessie was the one with enemies. Gobind had just been doing Jessie one last favour. He'd needed the money to help pay for Baby's tuition and then was going to tell Jessie he was out. But leaving the gang life behind wasn't the problem he'd imagined it would be; nothing was more useless to Jessie than a guy in a wheelchair.

Gobind and Jessie hadn't stayed in touch, but now there he was, suddenly in his life again—and this time, causing problems for Baby. Gobind thought he'd made himself clear after the Vegas rumours had surfaced; he'd reminded Jessie that he owed him, and as a personal favour, asked Jessie to stay away from Devi. But clearly he hadn't. People were still talking shit about Devi, and Baby was acting like none of it was real, because what choice did he have? The wedding had cost their family everything. Baby could hardly back out now. They'd be ruined. All of it made Gobind feel helpless. What good was an older brother if he couldn't protect his baby brother?

That morning as he lay in bed listening to the clatter of pots and pans, his mother and aunties preparing for the maiyan, he tried to remind himself of his good fortune, and recited some positive affirmations his father had sent him. But gratitude was a relative beast that always led him to think he was better than or less than someone else, so in a way he wondered if it was better to cleave himself from the past, accepting that he'd had one kind of life before the accident and another kind of life after the accident—full stop. Better to think of who he'd been before as some alternate-universe version of Gobind, and who he was after as who he always was. "This is my life," he said to himself as he started the work of moving himself out of his bed. Even though it had been years, he'd never gotten used to the way he had to prop, shift and shimmy his body out of bed and into his chair. He was relieved that Sonia was gone before he woke up each morning. He didn't want her to feel bad for him the way everyone else did. When he was with her, he felt like himself, the version of him that he was before the accident, before he'd ever met Jessie. When he was with her he felt alive and loved, but the minute she was gone he knew they couldn't really be together. She lived in Boston and her parents probably wouldn't allow it. There were a million reasons why it wouldn't work, and only one reason—as she'd reminded him last night—why it would work: she'd always loved him.

"You wouldn't love me if you knew what I'd done," he confessed.

"There's nothing you could tell me that would change how I feel about you."

With that reassurance, he told her about that night at the club and about having worked with Jessie. "I brought it on myself. It was no accident." Although he suspected that at least Baby knew the truth, he had never admitted it to anyone. He had never said it out loud, but her reaction, her instant forgiveness, made him feel like the luckiest man alive, even if only for a minute.

By the time he'd finished getting ready and made his way into the kitchen, he knew his well-meaning relatives would comment on his oversleeping, not understanding how much time it took him to move from A to B. He was glad he didn't have to use the lift to go upstairs very often; he hated how slowly it moved and how it seemed that everyone would stop what they were doing to watch him, all of them thinking what a sad and mechanical life he had and how glad they were to not be him. Sometimes he thought it was their pity that had kept him so stuck. The only person who didn't feel sorry for him was his mother. She never talked about what could or should have been; she dealt with life as it was.

His mother had had the lift installed before he was even dis-
charged from the hospital; she'd hired contractors to renovate
his bathroom. Meanwhile his father was sitting on a mountain
in India praying the paralysis away, when really he should have
been home with the family, adapting. But his father wasn't stoic
like his mother. Although Satnam never wept about the accident
in front of his sons, Gobind sometimes still heard him crying in
the shower, and saw how easily he was overcome, tears forming
in the corners of his eye like dewdrops. He hadn't been like that
before the accident. He was quiet and occasionally playful, the
kind of man who would put his hand on his son's shoulder in
a crowd, who would kick a ball around when he had time, who
would sit and read the paper while his sons watched cartoons
on a Saturday morning. He was still quiet, but now his silence
was a long shadow, something that followed him around telling
him to be careful, to watch for signs, to surrender to God. The
previous week when he'd given Gobind the business card of a
life coach he'd met in the taxi, Gobind hadn't been surprised.
His father was always looking for someone to make things better for him—and by better, he meant less paralyzed. Satnam had
already tried to send him to a hypnotist, a naturopath, a faith
healer, a shaman, a shrink and now a life coach, approaching his
condition as though it were some kind of mind-over-matter situation, something he could manifest his way out of. Not wanting
to argue with his father, he'd taken the card and told him he'd
make an appointment after the wedding even though he wasn't
going to. But now everything he felt for Sonia was making him
reconsider. She made him feel at ease, and made him want to
be better at the same time. Maybe talking to someone about his
future wasn't such a terrible idea. After the accident he'd only
ever been with his now ex-girlfriend, and the entire thing was

awkward and disappointing, so much so that when she broke it off with him weeks later, he wasn't even surprised. He thought she deserved better. He couldn't give her what she wanted, not in bed and not in life. Before the accident he was the guy that everyone—including women—wanted to be around. After the accident, he was just the guy in the wheelchair, the guy who'd had something bad happen to him, as opposed to the guy who made things happen. In his eyes, Sonia was the same but in reverse; although her body transformation was hardly equivalent, she knew what it was to be one thing and then another, but didn't need to talk about it endlessly. She could just be.

Sonia was thoughtful, especially on days like today, when the house was full of guests and his movements would be hampered by others. She scouted the perfect spot in the yard for him to watch the maiyan from, and forged a path for him so he wouldn't have to inch his way forward, nudging people out of the way—people who would turn toward him and then smile in that confused and apologetic way when they had to look down at him.

"It's going to start soon," Sonia said, standing behind him, her hand on his shoulder. "Are you sure you don't want to join in?"

He held her hand and shook his head. "Nah, I'm good." His mother had already asked him if he wanted to rub the turmeric paste into Baby's skin but he'd declined. He didn't want to hold things up, to have to wheel around the tightly packed yard, to have everyone's attention on him. It was Baby's day. "You go ahead. Let the cleansing begin."

From the sidelines, he watched his brother crouch down on a small stool, his feet planted on a wooden board in front of the colourful rangoli, and gave him a cheesy thumbs-up, but Baby was so focused that he didn't notice. Baby had been on edge for days, and the day before when Gobind had asked him if he still wanted to go through with it, he'd said he just needed space, and took a breath from his inhaler. Gobind knew that the house full of people, the constant noise, the demands of family and the attention—all of it was pressing in on Baby like it did when he was younger. Baby hadn't had an asthma attack for years. The first time it happened was when their parents had let them go unaccompanied to the PNE when they were kids. Out of nowhere, the swirling rides, the screams, the sounds of the carnival games, the smell of sugar and popcorn had Baby clutching his chest and dry-heaving over a garbage bin. "Just take a breath," Gobind had told Baby. "It'll be okay."

It's what Gobind had told Baby this morning after he and Devi had argued about the chair covers for the reception. She wanted pleated backs and their mother had ordered ones with silk bows. "She's never happy," Baby said, aware that the chair covers were simply a proxy for some larger discontent. He chucked his phone across the room. "If anyone should be pissed it's me!" Gobind had urged him to take a beat, to let it go. "It's just nerves. By this time tomorrow, you'll be married. It'll be over soon. Just remember to breathe."

The aunties and bibis sang folk songs, their strained voices piercing the air while Sonia and the California cousins held a phulkari canopy over Baby's head. As their relatives lined up to rub the paste into Baby's skin, Gobind focused in on Sonia, observing how quick she was to smile, to laugh, to join in. He loved that about her. There was a lot about her that he loved. When he was younger his parents were always joking about the two of them getting married, and now he could see why. They were a good match.

From beneath the shaded tree where he sat, Gobind watched his parents hand-feed Baby sweets and pose for pictures. After, his mother stepped over the rangoli several times before scooping up the remains, tossing them behind her and stamping her turmeric-stained palm on the wall for supposed good luck.

His father, always superstitious, had given Gobind a beaded bracelet he'd bought at a temple in India. It was meant to ward off the evil eye. Although Gobind wore it, he hated all the quasi-religious rituals that no one could really explain. As a child he wasn't supposed to eat meat on Tuesdays, got in trouble if he entered the house with his left foot and couldn't leave the house if someone had just sneezed, all of which was intended to preserve his luck. As he watched his mother mark the house with her palm prints, he realized that why things were done was not as important as the doing. So much of life was just the keeping of tradition; it was about doing the things that were expected, and now, because of his paralysis, so little was expected of him. All they wanted for him was happiness. There was some freedom in that.

YOU INDIANS ARE EVERYWHERE

Mrs. Richardson was not a racist. She simply liked things a certain way. She believed that God rested on Sunday and so too should people. She believed that rules were what kept societies functioning and ought to be respected. She believed that cleanliness was next to godliness. She supported immigration reform and the politics of making things "great again," even if it meant her seventeen-year-old granddaughter would not speak to her anymore. At seventy-seven, she was still as sharp as a tack, as her late husband George used to say, and though he'd been dead for almost ten years, she carried on as if he were still alive, doing all the things they would have done together, sometimes talking to him as if he were still there. "I told you this would happen. Didn't I?" she said, staring across the street at the Atwal house, which was a buzz of activity. "I told you his wedding would be a circus. I should have left town for the week when I saw those party tents go up." The Atwals' front door and columned entrance was draped in red and gold velvet and the

house was lit up like a Christmas tree, white string lights dripping from the fascia.

This would be the third time this year that her neighbourhood had become a spectacle. Tented guests in their colourful
traditional dress, children running around, loud music, catered
curry that surely would attract rats. Before the Indians arrived
there were never any rats, and now she had to put out traps
and keep her porch door closed in the summer just to be sure
that none would nest in her house the way they had in her shed.
Even now, as the sun crossed the sky, she could feel the heat
crawling through the house and felt trapped, a prisoner in her
own home.

She rifled through her stack of junk mail looking for
the invitation that Mrs. Atwal had left at the door weeks ago.
Flipping through the elaborate card, which had several events
listed, she wondered how many more days she'd be expected to
tolerate their loud bhangra music with its deep drumbeat and
heavy bass. Last summer one family three blocks away even had
fireworks. Would the Atwals have them as well? Wasn't it bad
enough that she'd had to suffer through the shrieking fireworks
of Diwali this past autumn? "Good grief, they just keep coming,"
she said as she watched guests park along their once quiet street.

"Stop being a fuddy-duddy," she heard George say. "You
should just go. They invited you."

Mrs. Atwal had invited all the neighbours, but unlike
Mrs. Haskill, who had borrowed an outfit from an Indian
co-worker to wear to the wedding, Mrs. Richardson had no
intention of going. "Why would I go to the wedding when I don't
even know them?" she'd told Mrs. Haskill, who'd been power
walking by the other day.

"To show support. Besides, it's fun to dress up and learn about another culture," Mrs. Haskill had said in her retired-kindergarten-teacher voice that made everything sound exciting. Mrs. Richardson scoffed, saying that she was too old to be playing dress-up and then Mrs. Haskill, who was pumping two-pound weights, went on and on about it not being appropriation, to which Mrs. Richardson shrugged, because she didn't know what appropriation was, only that Fox News thought it was woke nonsense.

"I'll call the city," she said to George. "They're probably breaking all kinds of rules, same way they do with all them zoning laws." For years she'd walked the same route around her neighbourhood—up and around Collingwood Street to 118th and across the park toward the rancher with the large oak tree and back again—but last week the white rancher with the green shutters and the Dutch door was hidden behind a blue construction fence. She'd stood at the front of the property reading the city rezoning notice. It would be the seventh house on her walking route to be demolished this year. At first, she'd been naive enough to believe that her numerous letters to city hall and her attendance at the municipal meetings would make a difference, but her long-time citizenship, her outrage and her concern were no match for what the city called "progress." She didn't understand how tearing down perfectly nice houses, uprooting mature trees and gardens and replacing them with these monster houses was progress, but there it was, another sign that her way of life was being stripped away. Most of the long-time residents like her had sold their homes, cashed out, moved east and downsized into gated golf communities, or moved to oceanfront homes in the Gulf Islands. She hadn't wanted to leave. She'd lived there her whole married life. Raised her family there. And now that

George was gone, where would she go? What would she retire to? Sometimes she thought of those early days, how her sons would race around the neighbourhood on their bikes, play in the sprinkler in the summer and have backyard tented sleepovers. The neighbourhood was their whole world, but now the world had come for their neighbourhood.

First it was just a few Indians, but now they were everywhere, with their mega-houses, extended families, cooking smells and fancy cars. Some had even taken to pulling up their front lawns to create more room for parking! She'd called the city's bylaw office countless times, reporting illegal suites, oversized backyard sheds, haphazard parking, but nothing had changed—and now this! "This noise, noise, noise. It's too much to bear," she said.

"You sound like the Grinch," George said.

"Hush now. I'm on hold." She waited, caught in an endless loop of options, none of which suited her. "If you know the extension of the person you are trying to reach, enter it now; otherwise, wait on the line for more options." She waited. "For business licenses, press one. For planning, press two. For traffic violations, press three. For parks and recreation, press four. For all other options, press five." She pressed five, and while she waited on hold she stared across the street, trying to estimate how many guests there were just in case the bylaw officer asked.

The Atwals had lived across from her for years but she'd never spoken to them, preferring to exchange an occasional head nod or wave when they happened to be out watering their lawn or collecting the mail at the same time. She'd felt bad about what happened to their older son but not enough to go over with a casserole. "Do Indian people even eat that?" she'd asked Mrs. Haskill, who'd gone over with two frozen lasagnas.

159

The hold music stopped.

"Hello, yes, my name is Margaret Richardson," she began, only to be interrupted by the automated message. "Thank you for holding. Please stay on the line. One of our agents will assist you." The easy jazz music began again, and small trumpets and soft percussion filled her ears as she poured herself a second cup of coffee. Then, suddenly: "Hello, this is Rajvinder. How may I help you?"

"Hello Virginia, this is—"

"Rajvinder," the woman on the phone said, correcting her without a hint of an accent. "My name is Rajvinder."

"Yes of course," Mrs. Richardson said, not repeating her name. "I'm calling to register a noise complaint."

"Certainly. Have you filled in the online form?"

"Well no. I haven't got a computer."

"Oh," Rajvinder said, slightly confused. "Is there someone that can fill it in for you?"

"Yes, you. Isn't that your job?"

"Not exactly. Let me transfer your call."

"No, wait—" Mrs. Richardson said, but before she could finish her sentence, that hold music was in her ear again. She shook her head and hung up the phone. "Progress," she said. "Can you believe that, George? You can't even talk to a real person anymore."

"Well actually you did," she heard him say. "You just didn't like what you heard."

"Hmm," she said, miffed. She looked over the top of her glasses at the parked cars lining both sides of the street, people spilling out of the tent and into the yard. A few nights ago, she'd called the police and complained about loud music, and even though they'd dispatched a car, the music continued, so she knew that if she called today about the rowdy partygoers and the cars blocking her driveway it would not be addressed. For the rest of the evening, she tried to busy herself with her usual routines—knitting, crosswords, sudoku—but her frustration could not be contained, and before she knew it she was standing under the Atwals' velvet-draped entrance, ringing the doorbell. No one answered, and it was only after she'd been waiting awhile that she noticed, taped to the column, a sign directing guests toward the backyard. She followed the sign around the house and into the backyard where another, larger tent, this one filled with dinner tables, had been set up beneath a canopy of lights. She stood there for a moment looking for Mrs. Atwal in the crowd of costumed and bejewelled women. They did look beautiful, almost regal, in their fine embroidered silks and gold jewellery, and suddenly she felt silly for barging in on their party, dressed in her pilled sweatpants and fleece vest. She was turning to leave when she heard Mrs. Haskill call her name. "Over here," she yelled over the music, patting the empty chair next to her. "I'm so glad you came." Mrs. Haskill was beaming. "Wait until you try the food. The pakoras are amazing."

"Oh no, I can't. Indian food doesn't agree with me."

"Oh how unlucky! You don't know what you're missing," Mrs. Haskill said, popping a baked fritter into her mouth. "So delicious."

Mrs. Richardson sat quietly, unsure of what she had even wanted to say to Mrs. Atwal, who was now making her way to their table.

"We are so happy you came to celebrate with us," Mrs. Atwal said.

Mrs. Richardson lowered her head slightly and pressed her palms together the way she'd seen Indian people do on TV.

"Thank you for inviting me," she said, feeling utterly ridiculous; she must have looked like she was bowing.

"Please, eat. Enjoy," Mrs. Atwal said, and then continued on greeting and thanking her guests.

"You're just in time," said Mrs. Haskill. "Soon they will perform a maiyan. It's a purifying ritual where they cleanse the groom's skin with yellow paste and sing folk songs. Apparently they did this once already. Can't be too clean, I guess! It's going to be just fascinating."

"I'm sure," Mrs. Richardson said, noting the way Mrs. Haskill said *fascinating* the same way one might when reading *National Geographic*.

"Yes, such a rich culture. So much ritual! You know it makes our weddings seem, well, boring."

"Well, all cultures have rituals. Christmas trees and Santa Claus, wedding veils and vows, church bells and trick-or-treaters. We have rituals . . . You're just so used to yours is all."

"I suppose," Mrs. Haskill said, looking at the bedazzled women longingly.

"Is that the other one?" Mrs. Richardson said, motioning toward Gobind, who was sitting on the sidelines.

"If you mean their other son, yes it is. Such a shame. He was such a sweet kid."

"Was? Is he no longer sweet?"

"Oh, no, I'm sure he is. I just meant about the accident. It's so unfair."

"Course it is," Mrs. Richardson said. "How would anything like that be fair? For Pete's sake."

"I just mean that it was so senseless."

"Indeed," said Mrs. Richardson, thinking about how senseless it was that she was here at this party and that it was her

George who would have enjoyed it—yet, here she was alone. "Is that his girlfriend?" she nudged Mrs. Haskill and pointed to a girl who was now standing behind Gobind, her hand resting on his shoulder as she leaned in to talk to him.

"I'm not sure," Mrs. Haskill said.

"She's a family friend," said a young woman who had just sat down in the empty seat across from them. "I'm Priya," the girl said, "a reporter from *Awaaz* magazine."

"A reporter from a-where?" Mrs Richardson asked.

"*Awaaz*," Priya clarified. "It's a local South Asian magazine."

Intrigued, Mrs. Haskill straightened up as if she were the one being interviewed.

"I cover events like this for our wedding edition, so I get to know who's who. Apparently everyone who is anyone will be at this wedding, even their member of parliament," Priya said with a hint of sarcasm that went over Mrs. Haskill's head.

"Incredible. I had no idea that the Atwals were such a prominent family, did you?" Mrs. Haskill turned toward Mrs. Richardson, who was no longer paying attention. She'd been watching Gobind and that girl, the quiet tenderness between them, the gentle way he placed his hand on hers, a moment that would only be noticed by those who had been in love the way she had been. It made her smile.

"Sonia and some of the other female relatives made the rangoli for the maiyan," Priya explained, detailing how the design was made and explaining that a similar event was unfolding at the bride's home.

Mrs. Haskill shifted in her seat to get a better look. "I can't wait to see this. Such a rich culture!"

"Rituals, tradition, ceremony, all of it is what gives our lives shape. We live by repeating," Mrs. Richardson said, remembering that George never got bored of doing the same things. But now nothing was the same. Not for her. "I think I'll be going now," she said, ignoring Mrs. Haskill's pleas for her to stay.

On her way out, Mrs. Richardson thanked Mrs. Atwal for inviting her.

"But you haven't eaten yet."

"I'm fine. I ate my supper already, but thank you."

"Will we see you at the wedding?"

"Oh, I'm afraid not, but maybe the next one," she said gesturing toward Gobind, who was whispering something in Sonia's ear that made her blush. "They make a nice couple."

Mrs. Atwal, who had been smiling, turned back toward Mrs. Richardson with a look of surprise and confusion on her face. "Oh no, they are just friends," she said and handed Mrs. Richardson a box of sweets. "Thank you again for coming."

Mrs. Richardson crossed the street back to her darkened house where she told George all about it. "Do you think I outed them? What if their parents don't know, or what if they've already been arranged to someone else?"

"Arranged? Woman, I think you've been watching too many of them docudramas."

"You're probably right," she said. "But their customs are so different."

"Different is good."

"George, you would've liked it. The music, the food—I swear I saw Mrs. Haskill putting sweets and samosas in her purse for later."

"Sounds like you should have stayed longer."

"Oh no, I don't belong there," she said as she got ready for bed.

"What about the fireworks? At least go watch those. You always loved watching those with the boys."

"Did I?"

When George didn't answer she got into their empty bed, thinking about the way that girl had looked at Gobind, and remembered how tenderly George always kissed her hand before he said good night.

Later, Mrs. Richardson stood on her front deck in her housecoat and slippers watching the explosion of colours, the spark and scattering of light across the night sky. She closed her eyes for a moment and listened to the bursts and blasts, the awe-filled crowd clapping and laughing. She tried to hold it all in—such joy. She'd wondered where it all went.

A GOOD FAMILY

NOW THAT MRS. RICHARDSON HAD POINTED IT OUT, BALBIR COULD not unsee it. How had she been so blind? Gobind and Sonia had been inseparable all week and she'd thought nothing of it, other than to think how nice it was to see them together again, talking and laughing just as they did when they were children. Yet now as she watched them sitting side by side, she saw the familiarity, the lingering glances, the softened edges of their interactions. Had she been so busy that she had not observed what Mrs. Richardson had seen straight away? She scanned the tent and wondered if any of her other guests had noticed, or if they were just like her, so absorbed in their own lives that they paid no mind to anyone else.

Though she was normally an observant person, the Dosanjhs had distracted her with their never-ending demands and drama. Her relatives had warned her that although the Dosanjh's were a good family they were not a *good* family; they had some questionable associations. At the time, she dismissed the idea that there were different types of good—and so what if they knew some unsavoury people, didn't everyone? But when her family was the target of their haughty condescension and classist remarks that purported blueberry farming was somehow above sweet making, when they'd insisted on venues and a guest list of over a thousand that they knew the Atwals could not afford and then opted to use a different sweet shop for their ladoo boxes, the difference became clear. And that was before the matter of the disgusting rumour about Devi, which out of respect, she never even mentioned—even though she knew they would not have done the same if the rumours were about her son. There were families that looked good, and those that *were* good. Devi's family, with their big house and fancy cars, was nice to look at, but Sonia's family was nice. Her parents, Gurmaan and Veero, had always been such loyal and supportive friends; perhaps a relationship between Gobind and Sonia would be a blessing. After everything her family had been through, didn't they deserve that?

The idea filled her with hope, and when the bhangra started she was the first one on the dance floor, urging her wallflower of a husband to join her. She could not recall the last time they had danced with such abandon, and as time went on she kicked off her shoes and twirled around and around like she'd done when she was a schoolgirl. As she watched Satnam attempt to hop up and down in a squat, she was reminded of how he'd surprised her these last few months. He had worked without complaint to make this wedding happen for Baby, and in that moment it inspired in her the kind of love she'd had for him when they'd first settled in Canada and started their business. They'd had nothing, yet everything was possible. How joyful life was when you had nothing to lose. She'd always blamed her pragmatism on Satnam's propensity for mysticism, but perhaps a little faith was just what she needed now. She reached for Satnam, who was struggling in his squat, about to topple, and helped him up. They circled the dance floor once more before finally encouraging their guests to form a single line for the finale dance to "Rail Gaddi." Satnam moved slowly at first, acting as the train's engine, picking up steam when the song's whistle blew. Behind him, guests cheered and chugged along, pumping their arms like pistons, singing about their train arriving, and indeed, Balbir felt that it had.

What more could she want? She was surrounded by her family, her friends and neighbours. All of this they had built from nothing. It was Satnam who had wanted to move to Canada, not Balbir. She'd been happy in India; she had friends and family, a job she liked, and their life—though small—had a routine that suited her. But Satnam wanted something better for the children they'd eventually have and so they'd set out, leaving everyone they loved behind. She'd never thought about what that would mean for her. She did not return to India for many years, and when she did it was for her father's funeral. She'd been too young to understand that making a better life for her children would mean a much harder life for her.

It was eleven p.m. by the time the party was winding down. Dinner had been served and cleared and the remaining guests were gathered in the front yard for the fireworks, and Balbir, who rarely drank, had downed three glasses of champagne in the last hour and was working on her fourth. She had so much to celebrate, and toasted the air. Her youngest son was getting married in the morning; her present financial worries could all be settled within a year if their frozen sweets venture took off—and as she looked at Gobind, who was talking to Sonia, she felt hopeful that perhaps he too could find some happiness.

After his accident, Balbir's life had stopped. Everything she'd ever wanted, everything she'd planned for was gone. In the early days, when Gobind was depressed and unresponsive, when the gravity of his situation caused him to wish he was dead—though it pained her, she'd understood. The life he'd had was gone and his body was a constant reminder. For years they lived in that rubble, just trying to survive, to stay together, to keep moving forward even if only toward a shapeless future, a mirage of something better. While her husband fell into spirituality and religion, she pulled their family from the ruins. They could not dwell in what was; they could not live on faith. She built up their business so they could afford all that they needed, and now here they were on the eve of Baby's wedding, at what felt like a new beginning for all of them.

As the fireworks lit up the sky she clinked glasses with Sonia's mother, Veero, who was now standing next to her. "To our children," Balbir said, motioning to Gobind and Sonia, who were standing on the other side of the street watching the night sky fill with light. "They seem so happy together."

"They always were."

"Yes, but now it seems like something more, doesn't it? We always said they were well-suited." Sonia had crouched down next to Gobind and was nuzzling his cheek playfully. Balbir waited for Veero to say something, but she remained quiet. "Remember when they were younger and we talked about how wonderful it would be if they were a match? Our two families becoming one?"

"Yes, but they were just children and, well, that was before—"

"Before what?" Balbir turned to look directly at Veero.

Veero did not return her gaze. "I just meant that it was a long time ago. Things were different."

"Different how?"

Veero stammered and stopped. "Phenji, would you really have me say it?"

"Yes, just so I'm clear on your meaning."

"Things were different before the accident."

"Ah, there it is," she said, nodding slowly. "So, because he's in a chair he's not good enough for your daughter anymore." Her voice was ripe with indignation.

"It's got nothing to do with him," Veero said, raising her voice above the din of the blasts above.

"It's got everything to do with him. With us. We treated you like family," Balbir said and started to walk away. "You know, after the wedding, I think you should go."

"Go where?"

"To hell for all I care," she said, flinging her arm in the air, spilling her champagne.

"Come now, you don't mean that. You've had too much to drink. If the situation were reversed, you'd feel exactly the same way," Veero said, calling her back.

Balbir turned, lowering her voice when she saw that other guests had noticed their shouting. "No, I would not."

"Yes, you would. No one wants their daughter to have to take care of a man; they want a man to take care of their daughter."

"I would never have raised a daughter that needed to be taken care of."

"Look, if anyone should understand, it's you. You've always been the sensible one. I'm just being practical. Life is hard enough without the added burdens."

"And my son is the burden?"

"I didn't mean it like that," she said, her voice fading like the sparks above. "Don't be angry with me. I just imagined . . . I just wanted something different for Sonia."

Balbir turned her attention to the sky, now filled with smoke. "We all wanted something different once." She too had wanted so much for her children—good grades, good friends, good schools, a good education, a good job, a good wife, a good life; the older they got the longer her wish list became. All her wants were for them; every desire and every thought she had were ideas she set in orbit, as if she, like some deity, could create their future the way she'd created their lives. No wonder she had become so confused by what she could and could not control. No wonder some days she woke up spiralling in what should be.

THE BRAMPTON
BRIDE'S ADVICE

A S JAG HEADED EAST ON THE DESOLATE HIGHWAY TOWARD DEVI'S house, the sun still low on the horizon, she felt like the only person alive. The air was unusually thick; she rolled down the window, but the breeze only deepened the humidity and snapped her senses to some other moment, some other life. She'd felt that same heaviness in her chest fifteen years ago in Brampton, when, lying in bed with her then-husband, the ceiling fan whirring overhead, she'd realized she had to leave him. What an escape it had been. Not planned, the way they'd said it was. She was no great manipulator—as the news stories claimed—for if she had been, she would have emptied the bank account instead of just the family safe. What good were a few bars of gold, her wedding jewellery and two hundred dollars from her husband's wallet? She hadn't even thought through the details until she'd driven a few hundred kilometres away and the sun was peeking over the horizon. It was then that she'd remembered how her co-workers at the Airport Inn had made extra cash to send back home each summer. Cottage country, they'd called it. She bought a gas station map and headed north. There she worked as a cleaner for a small resort along Georgian Bay. The old caretaker with the white beard and John Deere hat paid her fifty dollars a day and provided room and board in a broken-down cabin five kilometres inland. He hadn't asked her any questions and she'd provided no story. She wasn't a natural liar. That took time.

No one but her knew the true story, and sometimes she'd tell it to herself when she was alone so she wouldn't forget—but now, with so much time and so much life having gone by, she could hardly believe that she was ever that naive girl, and maybe that was for the best. The papers had called her the Brampton Bride, and their one-sided accounts had focused only on her thievery, never once investigating why a girl from India might have stolen away in the night only a few months after having arrived in the country.

Soon after her wedding, her husband admitted that he was in love with someone else and had only married Jag to keep his parents happy. He wasn't even apologetic about it. He didn't even try to hide his ongoing affair with the white woman. Why would he, when everyone was so willing to not see? When she asked him if he ever thought of how she might feel, he simply said, "I made the only choice I could." She understood that the alternative for him was being disowned, disgraced and exiled, or worse, alone—all the things that she would be if she made a fuss. She didn't even know how the immigration process worked. If she left him, would she be sent back to India? And if she did, what would her parents say? What would people say? She couldn't stay, she couldn't go home; her only option was to run away. She'd been disappearing her whole life. "That's what women do," her bibi once told her. "You just tuck yourself away and do what needs doing to get by."

Thankfully, back then lives were not lived online, and after a few news stories in the Indo-Canadian papers, her story disappeared. The Brampton Bride became nothing but an urban legend, an arranged-marriage gold-digger story.

She rolled up the window and turned the AC vents toward her face, trying to stay alert on the long stretch of highway flanked by farmland. Devi had texted the directions but Jag didn't need them. She, like everyone, knew where the house was; you could see the McMansion, with its limestone facade, gabled roof and roman columns from the highway. A monstrosity, that's what Pavan used to call it, and as Jag drove by the Blueberry King billboard toward the exit, she couldn't help but be reminded of all the mega-houses she'd cleaned when she worked for her at Clean and Tidy.

She was twenty-one by the time she'd saved enough money to move out west and start over. She'd arrived on the Greyhound with her one carry-on bag, a new name, fake ID and just enough money to rent a motel room for two months. Her neighbours came and went by the hour and for the most part she kept to herself, talking to no one but the Indian family that ran the place. She called them Auntie and Uncle. They had an eleven-year-old son with thick glasses, unruly, dandruff-flaked hair and the beginnings of a moustache. Bored and friendless, he became her self-appointed guide, showing her how to format a resumé and how to apply for jobs online. When she was almost out of money and prospects, a woman she met at the employment centre told her about Clean and Tidy. The owner, Pavan, once divorced herself, didn't pry into Jag's life the way the motel family did. She never asked her what village she was from, what she was studying, if she was married, nor did she try to pay her under the table or less than the going rate. She was kind but reserved;

the sort of person who had secrets and could keep them. All of the workers at Clean and Tidy were like that, hiding in plain sight, just like she was. Jag came to believe that everything in life happened for a reason; had she not worked for Pavan, she would never have met her future roommate, Hana. Hana was a Korean international student and a self-taught YouTube makeup artist who worked part-time at Clean and Tidy. Jag and Hana split the rent on a small basement suite, shed the hard edges of their accents by watching reruns of *Grey's Anatomy* and scrapped enough money together to start their own business.

Jag turned into the Dosanjhs' private tree-lined road and into the driveway that wound around a tiered marble fountain. The house was even larger up close, palatial in design, yet out of place amid the acres of farmland—especially with the red carpet that led to the front door and the swags of silk and roses that draped around the columned portico. Inside, the house was festooned with vibrant silk canopies, botanical garlands and ornamental lanterns that transformed the grand entrance into something out of a movie. Devi's mother, Raman, still in her robe and curlers, motioned for Jag to go on upstairs. "Oh and give Devi this, will you?" she said, handing her a hot water bottle.

"Thank God!" Devi said, snatching the water bottle from Jag. She tore off her woolen socks and rolled her feet over the hot water bottle one at a time, explaining how her feet were so stiff that it seemed all her bones and tendons had been replaced with steel joints. "I feel like the fucking tin man from *The Wizard of Oz*," she said, placing the hot water bottle on top of her feet. "They've been like this all morning. I didn't know what to do so I called my best friend and bridesmaid, Yazmin—who happens to be a nurse—and told her my feet were like ice, and she said,

'That's normal, it's wedding day nerves, cold feet,' and I'm like, No . . . they are *literally* cold. I cannot feel a fucking thing."

"Has this ever happened before?" Jag asked, knowing that when it came to brides on their wedding day, it was best to just go with whatever they were feeling.

"When I was a kid. I'd feel all iced up and get intestinal pop rocks before public speaking. Once I couldn't even move," she said, recounting her fifth-grade play. "I was the lead and I just, froze . . . *literally*, I could not even walk off stage. They had to carry me. Oh my God! What if that happens today?"

"It won't. Trust me, I see this sort of thing all the time," Jag said, reassuring her. "You're just exhausted, and rightly so. Planning a wedding is a lot."

"It is, isn't it?" Devi sighed. "Finally someone who gets it." She hobbled into her walk-in closet and came out wearing her red lehenga blouse and sweatpants. She turned her back so Jag could do up the hooks. "Is it terrible that I just want it to be over?"

"No, that's pretty normal. This is the last thing to check off your list before you start your new life."

"My new life." She whispered it as if she was making peace with the idea. "That makes sense."

"Why don't we get started?" Jag said and patted the chair that Devi would be sitting in for the next two hours. Usually brides had an entourage on their wedding day, but Devi had requested that Jag send Hana and her team of stylists to her bridesmaids so she could get ready in private. She wanted a reveal. Even Rish wasn't invited to document the process of getting ready that so many girls were posting on socials.

For most of the morning Devi was quiet and Jag was glad to not have to make the small talk that most brides needed. Having spent so much time with Devi already, she didn't think she could listen to another cycle detailing how she'd met Baby and all the reasons she loved him.

"Look up. To the right," Jag said as she touched up Devi's eyeliner. "Now close your eyes. Try not to move."

Devi's eyes were like butterflies. "I'm sorry, I'm just nervous."

"Of course you are. Just take a breath," Jag said, inhaling and exhaling slowly. "How are your feet? Any better?"

Devi wiggled her toes. "A little."

"Can you close your eyes again? This time try to focus on one spot in the darkness," she said, wand in hand. "That's good, nearly done." She cleaned up the edge and capped the liner. "Perfect."

"Why haven't you gotten married?" Devi asked, in a way that suggested she thought all women ought to be married.

"I don't know. I guess it never felt like the right time," Jag said as she looked through her case for the setting spray.

"What about your partner? Doesn't she want to get married?"

"No, we're good as we are." Jag avoided the sharing of personal details that women barter with to gain favour or connection, details that they later use against each other. Her partner, Rachel, did want to get married, but Jag didn't, not even after they had their son. Of the two of them, Rachel was the more maternal. At first she thought it was because Rachel had carried him, but later Jag realized that she just wasn't the nurturing type. She couldn't get close the way Rachel did. Rachel's parents had been married for forty years. She had siblings who loved her. She had people she could count on—yoga friends, drinking friends, work friends, high school friends—so many people. Rachel had never had to keep a secret; she didn't understand how one pulled thread could unravel it all. For Jag, the idea of getting married again was that thread.

"Independent women."

"Something like that," she said as she glossed Devi's lips.

"I never thought I'd get married . . . yet here I am, doing what's expected."

"It's normal to have second thoughts," Jag said, aware that Devi had checked her phone messages several times, the way one does when they're waiting for news. "A marriage is a big decision. You have to be sure, or at least as sure as you can be."

"That's the problem," she said, wringing her hennaed hands. "I'm sure I love Baby—but I'm not so sure I should marry him." She paused. "Remember that rumour I told you about?"

"About the guy in Vegas?"

"Yeah."

"What about it?"

"Well, he and I . . . We hooked up." Her eyes were suddenly wide with panic. "Oh my God, I can't believe I told you. You won't tell anyone will you?"

"Of course not," Jag said, crossing her heart. "Stylist-client confidentiality."

"You must think I'm a terrible person."

"Not at all. No judgments here."

She exhaled. "It was just the one time . . . but I feel awful about it. I think I have to tell Baby."

"No, you don't have to tell him anything," Jag said, putting her makeup brush down.

"But I cheated, he deserves to know. Even Dear Auntie thinks so."

"Dear Auntie? Puh-lease, you can't listen to her. She's a fraud."

"You know who she is?"

"Stylist-client confidentiality, remember . . . but I swear she doesn't know what she's talking about."

"And you do?"

"Yeah, I do, and I don't think you should tell him—not if you love him. Not if you want to marry him. Do you? Want to marry him."

"Yes, more than anything."

"Then you can never tell him the truth. He'd never forgive you for it."

"Well then what am I supposed to do?"

"Live with the lie."

"How?"

"You just have to forget about it." Jag thought about the identity she'd constructed for herself, the life she'd made with Rachel. By the time they'd met, Jag was a seasoned liar and told her a half truth, admitting only that she'd come to Canada to get married but that it fell through. She pretended that her old life was someone else's. "Lie to yourself and then you'll learn to believe it."

"Are you sure?"

Jag recognized the fear in Devi's eyes. It was the same look children got when they were lost in a crowd, spinning around for a friendly face and hand to hold. "Believe me. If you tell him the truth, you may feel better, but he'll never trust you again. Besides, everyone deserves a fresh start." Jag spun Devi around so she could see the bride she had become. "And your fresh start is now."

What she didn't tell Devi was that fresh starts were never clean. Even now, when curiosity got the better of Jag, she looked up her ex on Facebook. He was married to the woman he'd been having an affair with. They had two children. One boy, one girl. She scrolled through his picture-perfect life of Disney cruises and European vacations. She liked to think it had all worked out for the best. She'd since cashed in the gold bars she'd stolen and pawned all her wedding jewellery, with the exception of the one modest bracelet her bibi had given her. Occasionally, she thought about melting it down and making something for Rachel, but she hadn't been able to let it go.

COLD FEET

AS SOON AS DEVI TOLD JAG ABOUT JESSIE SHE REGRETTED IT, AND SHE was glad when Jag left; she didn't want to be around someone who knew what she'd done. She hadn't told anyone else, not even her best friend, Yazmin. Deny, deny, deny. This was what she had learned from her family—so why she had felt the need to suddenly unburden herself, she could not say. Perhaps it was the physical proximity to Jag, this woman who smelled like spring and crisp mountain air and was free from everything. Unmarried. Unbothered. Unconventional. Devi wanted that too. She wanted everything, and maybe it was this closeness to someone so different than her that made her open up and tell the truth, and maybe it was for those very same reasons that she'd gotten involved with Jessie in the first place.

Jessie hadn't replied to any of the messages she'd sent him saying that it was over, and she didn't know how to interpret his silence. She'd regretted having sex with him almost as soon as it started. She had hoped he would be a ramrod of a fuck, the kind that made you feel wanted and used, the kind that made you feel powerful and helpless all at the same time, but their rhythm was entirely off. Aside from their first kiss and his first push into her, it was underwhelming and performative. Maybe Jessie had watched too much porn, or maybe he actually believed that she'd wanted all the things she'd said she did in their late-night calls, but regardless, now that she'd had him, she knew that Baby was the one she wanted. Jag was right. There was no point in telling him. It would ruin everything.

Devi inhaled and turned to examine her no-carbs flat abs in the mirror as she finished getting dressed. Her custom-made lehenga, which had taken weeks to hand embroider, fit perfectly. When she'd picked it up from the store, Uncleji said it had taken five women to embroider the red skirt and another two to bead the bodice and trim with Swarovski crystals. It was one of a kind, he assured her, even better than the one Priyanka Chopra wore. The wedding lehenga weighed over twenty pounds and had three full crinolines. Her double-strand Kundan necklace, head chain and tikka were set with real emeralds, and her stilettos were hand dyed and beaded to match the lehenga. The entire look was perfect, just as Devi had planned, yet now that it was on her body, it felt like a cage.

"Oh my God, Devi!" her mother said from the doorway. "You look so beautiful."

"Thanks." Devi couldn't take her eyes off herself.

"I brought you tea." Raman handed Devi a mug, which she refused. "You should have something. When was the last time you ate?"

"I can't, Mom. I don't think I can stomach it."

"It's just nerves."

"Apparently," Devi muttered, watching as her mother gathered and folded the pleats of her chunni. "Did you steam it first?"

"Of course," she said, draping it over her shoulder.

"Where's Suneet? Isn't she supposed to be doing this?"

"She texted that she's running late."

"Great," Devi said, shaking her head. "So much for hiring experts from Fancy Fashions."

"Relax, she'll be here soon. Everything will be fine."

"Yeah, I know," Devi said, annoyed at her mother's mothering. "Is Rish here?"

"Yes, he's just unloading his equipment."

"And what about the caterers? Are they at the temple already?"

"Of course."

"And did Jot check on the flowers?"

"Yes," Raman said. "Everything is taken care of. Just try to enjoy your day." She arranged the chunni on Devi's shoulder.

Devi nodded, though she wasn't sure she could enjoy anything. Nothing felt the way it should, and she knew she'd brought it on herself, but all she wanted was to blame someone else. Who better than a mother? "Ouch, careful with the pins."

"Hold still," Raman said, sewing the fabric in place the same way she used to stitch Devi's doll clothes.

"Were you this nervous on your wedding day?"

Raman nodded. "I was so young. I didn't know what to expect." She held the needle in her mouth as she fanned the pleats across Devi's chest. "Oh, Suneet makes this look so easy." She stitched and unstitched, trying to get the folds right.

"Did you want to get married?"

"I don't know what I wanted then. My mother had died and I did what my father told me to do. But you, you have the freedom to make your choices."

"You had choices."

"Not good ones," she said. "Things were different then. I've made peace with it and so should you."

"I just never understood why."

"It's not for you to understand."

"Sorry I'm late," Suneet said, rushing in. "I'll take over, Auntie." Suneet pulled the loose threads and restitched the chunni to the shoulder of Devi's top, anchoring it there before draping it across her chest like a sash. As Suneet pinned, sewed, steamed and folded everything in place, she gushed about how beautiful Devi looked. "Just a few more pins," she said, and attached the second red chunni to Devi's bun, pulling the cascading train behind her shoulders. "Perfect." She stood back when Rish came in to take photos.

"How about a few pictures of mother and daughter?" Rish asked.

Devi nodded, and she and her mother smiled and laughed, pretending that they were both in on the same jokes, as if this day was the happiest day of their lives. Devi wondered if it was, and whether she would know if it was before it was over. So much of life was only understood in hindsight. Was that how her mother felt about her own life, her own marriage? Devi had never told anyone other than Baby about her father's abuse, and even if she had no one would've believed that her father—who was now so thin and frail, who was kept and cared for by his wife—could have been anything but timid. Even she found it hard to believe that he was ever that person. Deny. Deny. Deny.

Rish asked her to stand by the window and look outside. Her chunni and jewellery were so heavy that her neck dipped forward under the strain; she hoped this slight angle would register as serenity in the pictures. Devi had been planning and preparing for this day for more than eighteen months, every detail painstakingly mapped out on Pinterest boards and work-back schedules. The bridesmaids' shararas with floral embroidery were custom-made in India; the groomsmen's raw-silk pocket squares and head scarves were hand dyed; the live band for the baraat was flown in from New York. Baby's arrival on a white horse, the colour-coordinated fresh floral garlands for the milini, the elaborate breakfast menu with five types of pastries, three types of parathas, pakoras, fresh fruit, yogourt parfaits, rice pudding and assorted sweets—all of it and more had been chosen by Devi—every detail an expression of her. "That's so me," she'd said when picking out decor and textiles, never once wondering if she could actually be embodied by a thing or if a thing could embody her. She wondered if that was why she had been feeling so outside of her body this morning—cold and numb with pin-pricked skin and flooding nausea. Was she nothing more than a collection of the things she wanted? Was this desire to have more, and never having enough a disease or a personal failing? A fever spread across her chest, her limbs iced up, her throat thickened and her legs almost gave out. "I need some air," she said, and despite her mother's protest, she teetered out of the room, rushed down the stairs and out of the house.

GOD WILLING

At eighty years old, Darshan had outlived most of her immediate family. Her husband, though still alive, was in a home and required full-time care and countless machines just to keep his heart from stopping. After multiple strokes, he'd become a husk of a man with clouded eyes that lived in the dreaming. Because she loved him, she was ashamed to say that she was relieved when his wordless grunts and gestures stopped. Nothing was worse than hearing a man suffer. Men were not built for it. She knew his time would come, as would hers, and all she wanted before she died—God willing—was to see her granddaughter get married. But now, just a few hours before the wedding, Devi had gone missing.

"Who let her leave?" Darshan asked.

"No one *let* her leave." Raman was defensive. "She said she needed some air and then she never came back."

"Has anyone checked where she likes to walk, in the fields."

"She's not there," Jot said. "I just checked again."

"What about her phone?"

"She doesn't have tracking on," he said. "But her car is gone."

"I can't believe this," Darshan said, turning to Raman. "How can you lose your own daughter on her wedding day?"

"No one lost anyone," Jot said, before they could get into it. "Knowing Devi, she's just being dramatic. I'm sure she'll be back any minute."

"Maybe, but we can't take any chances." Darshan checked the time. "You should all head to the gurdwara for the milini. Greet the boy's family, pretend everything is normal. I'll find Devi and bring her to the temple."

"But how?" Jot asked.

"Don't worry about that. You just go," Darshan said. "I think I know where to find her." She remembered that when Devi was a child her favourite place to go when she was feeling down was McDonald's. She thought that buying a Happy Meal would make her happy, and it usually did.

As the family made their way outside, Darshan hollered to the driver to start one of the Rolls-Royce limousines that Devi had insisted on renting and climbed inside. As they drove away, Darshan took a deep breath to curb her own frustration. After all the meticulous planning, she'd expected that Devi would have been happy—maybe even grateful—but clearly she was neither, and this pained Darshan, because in her day brides were not allowed to be happy. When she'd gotten married, her mother told her to keep her covered head down during the ceremony; all she'd seen of her own wedding were people's feet. When she raised her eyes ever so slightly she could catch legs and torsos or the smiling face of a child, but she never saw her husband, not until her wedding night, and then she'd been too shy to look at him. Even in the nights and months that followed, she felt ashamed that she liked sex, and that she, unlike all her newly married friends, had no complaints to make. Seva was a good man, but he had never been enough for her. What she wanted more than love was respect and power—in this way she and Devi were alike.

When she found her granddaughter sitting in the local McDonald's, eating an Egg McMuffin and being mistaken for a Disney princess by little girls who asked to take her picture, she wanted to tell Devi all of this. She wanted to tell her that she too had been young, she too had wanted and been wanted, she too had been lost in some nameless pursuit, but to what end? She wanted to tell her so many things—but no one wanted the musings of an old woman. Darshan knew that's how most people saw her. She was not blind to their polite and staid greetings, their convenient excuses that hastened the ends of conversations. She was an old woman, and she knew that when you were a woman and when you were old, that was all you were. To young people she was a nuisance, someone without history or consequence, and someone they had to tolerate to please the elders in their own homes, who also had no history or consequence. As far as Darshan was concerned, Devi was the only one who did not see her this way. Devi did not infantilize her the way some people did by saying how cute she was, how adorable she was—Devi would never have dared such disrespect.

Darshan bought a black coffee and slid into the plastic chair across from Devi.

"Everyone's worried." Darshan said, shooing away those who were taking videos of Devi to post on their socials. "What's going on?"

"Nothing. I'm fine."

"Devi, *this* is not fine. You should be at the temple by now."

"I know. I just needed some air and some food," she said, stuffing a hashbrown into her mouth. "I'm starving."

"So it seems . . . Wait until you try the food at the temple. It's better than anything you've ever tasted, even better than the Hotel Vancouver's restaurant. Remember, I took you there for your tenth birthday?" When Darshan was young, she and her sister-in-law, Jasvir, worked there as dishwashers; when Darshan returned home after her shift, she'd cook and clean for the family. Her father-in-law never had a kind word. He'd holler obscenities at her when his dinner was cold, or his dhal was too spicy, throwing his plate on the ground and blaming her for the mess. Years later, when he was old and sick, Darshan was purposeful in her neglect and let him marinate in his own filth. She was glad to let Jasvir take care of him while she took the only thing he'd ever loved—his money.

Even though boys were preferred in the Dosanjh family, Darshan adored her granddaughter. When Devi was born, Darshan's mother-in-law went into mourning. "What use is a girl?" she'd said of her great-granddaughter. Darshan's mother-in-law was a beastly woman, humourless and miserable, self-hating the way women with a small amount of power could be. Darshan told herself that she would never be like that, but she was powerless against it; the only way to endure was to adapt, to armour up, to cut down others before they cut you down. Like Darshan, Devi was a survivor; she would never be a victim the way her mother, Raman, had been, always crying over her situation instead of taking control of it.

"So now that you've eaten and had your *air*, do you want to tell me what's really going on?" Darshan asked. "We didn't raise you to run away from your problems."

"I don't know . . . I guess I'm just scared. I don't want to be like my mother. I don't want to be unhappy the way my parents are."

"You aren't your mother, and Baby, he is nothing like your father. I love my son, but I know his shortcomings. Your father, he is like your great-grandfather—born mean. But not all men are this way." Darshan took a sip of her coffee. "Besides, you aren't the type of person to just let things happen to you. You never have been! You will make your own happiness . . . and no matter what I said about Baby in the past, I know he's a good boy. You'll be happy with him."

Devi slurped her orange juice and nodded, as if she were trying to convince herself. "But I don't deserve Baby. I've treated him badly and I've done things I'm not proud of."

Darshan shook her head and held up her hand to signal that Devi needn't explain. She'd heard the stories about Jessie and she didn't want to hear them from Devi. "People make mistakes. It doesn't mean you don't deserve happiness. Whatever happened is not your fault." As far as Darshan was concerned, Jessie was to blame. He'd probably forced himself on her. He'd manipulated her the same way he'd manipulated Jot when he'd loaned him money for the farm and asked for favours in return. When they'd paid the loan back in full and told Jessie that he wouldn't be using their trucks anymore, Jessie had threatened them. With their backs against the wall, Darshan had led him to believe that they'd fallen in line and it was business as usual. But Jessie's mistake in all their dealings was that he'd underestimated Darshan; there was nothing she would not do for her family, for Devi. Their family honour was everything.

After the wedding, Darshan would make enquiries abroad. She would see to it herself, taking care of things as she always had.

"Everything will be fine, child," she said, patting Devi on the hand. "I promise. Soon you won't even remember feeling this way."

"Really?"

Darshan vowed that she was sure of it. Devi would be free of the past, free to live happily.

"I'm sorry. I feel so foolish," Devi said. "I didn't mean to worry anyone." Her eyes were welling up. "I'm so stupid. I've thrown the whole day off schedule, and Rish was supposed to take our leaving-the-house photos."

"Now, now, don't cry, you'll ruin your makeup. Besides, if we hurry, we'll still make it on time and we can take some pictures at the temple. Come now," she said, extending her hand to Devi the same way she did when Devi was a little girl and her feet did not yet touch the ground.

———

BY THE TIME DARSHAN AND DEVI ARRIVED AT THE TEMPLE, THE GROOM'S family—who was late—was still making their way down the adjacent street in their procession. Devi had applied for a permit to have the roads blocked so that Baby, on his white horse, could make a grand entrance. As a crowd gathered, the dhol drums grew louder, signalling the groom's approach. Devi's bridesmaids surrounded the limousine and whisked her away while Darshan joined the others to witness the baraat that had just turned the corner. Two drummers dressed in red and gold achkans led the procession, followed by trumpeters and chimta players. Baby—with his red turban, embroidered sherwani and tidy beard—looked princely riding through the crowd as his family danced around him. When they arrived at the temple gate, Baby dismounted for the short prayer that preceded the milini. Devi had not wanted the milini to be reserved for men and had arranged for all family members to exchange garlands with their counterparts, starting with Darshan, who—as the Dosanjh matriarch—embraced an Atwal elder. Bhajan then exchanged garlands with Satnam, Raman with Balbir, Gurjot with Gobind and Jasvir with Veero. On and on it went, each family member meeting their equivalent, with the men occasionally delighting the crowd as they tussled in an embrace, trying to best the other by picking them up off the ground. With the families acquainted, breakfast was served and guests chatted happily as they sampled the endless choices at the buffet.

In the near distance, Darshan saw her sister-in-law, Jasvir. They had practically grown up together before they grew apart, and now here they were as old women. What good was time if it only separated you from the people you were, the people you loved? Darshan wondered what might have to happen for them to reconcile, to make their family whole again, and approached Jasvir, embracing her fully.

"Vadayaan, Phenji," Jasvir said, pulling away from the embrace. "Everything is beautiful. Everything is as it should be."

"Suchee," Darshan said, accepting her blessings. She thought of Devi—who only an hour ago had been missing—and congratulated herself on making sure everything worked out, just as she always had.

DARSHAN HAD NOT EXPECTED TO CRY DURING THE CEREMONY. SHE HAD not cried when her own son was born, when he got married or when her husband had a stroke. Even her parents had boasted that as a child she had hardly whimpered, and now, here, at eighty years old, she could not stop sobbing. It was the sight of her granddaughter standing in front of the Guru Granth Sahib with her soon-to-be husband that broke her. They were beautiful. Him in his cream embroidered sherwani and her in her custom bejewelled lehenga, called back to some other honour-filled era. Darshan wiped her tears away with the back of her hands, and even as the ceremony continued and Devi's misstep had her start to lead the first laavaan rather than follow, and even when some laughed at this while others applauded it, Darshan was still crying.

Over the next hour, she watched her granddaughter circle the Guru Granth Sahib four times, and with every turn she saw everyone she'd ever loved embodied in that child, that girl, that woman. Unknowingly, Devi carried—as they all had—their ancestors' hopes and dreams for a new beginning, something better. God willing.

IZZAT

ALL OF SATNAM'S PRAYING HAD WORKED. BABY AND DEVI WERE MAR-
ried, and from what his wife, Balbir, had told him about
Sonia, perhaps Gobind would be next. He'd always liked her,
and he already suspected that she would be a much more dutiful
daughter-in-law than Devi. Satnam couldn't help but smile at
the idea of both of his sons married and settled, having children
of their own one day—what more could a man want? Per Devi's
instructions, he'd rented a tuxedo for the reception, and as he
walked around the reception talking to his guests he felt like he
was the star on a film set. Devi's "old Bollywood" theme, with
its black and white linens, crystal candelabras and red roses,
was sophisticated, and made Satnam feel like the great Amitabh
Bachchan. Arms raised, Satnam was victorious when he and
Balbir made their grand entrance, followed by Devi's parents,
followed by Baby and Devi who received—as they should—a
standing ovation. Gobind made a heartfelt speech, as did Devi's
brother, Jot, and then came dinner and the first dance. Having
seen so many first dances that looked like a high school hugging

one-step, Devi had insisted that she and Baby take ballroom dance lessons. Watching them waltz was as thrilling as anything Satnam had seen on the silver screen; they held each other with such majesty and care, swaying and twirling to and fro without ever breaking their gaze. In those moments, their love was palpable, and everyone at the reception felt it. Women instinctively put their hands on their hearts and men looked on longingly, wishing—as Satnam was—that they too could be the centre of a woman's affections. As he looked over at Balbir, he couldn't recall the last time they'd held one another like that. Their life had been one of holding each other up, not of holding on. He reached for her hand, kissed it and held it victoriously as if to say, We did this. Their love was in the doing.

After the first dance, the bridal party surprised Baby and Devi with a bhangra flash mob, inviting guests to join them until everyone was swept up in the dhol beat, including Satnam. After one turn on the dance floor, he stood back and watched the celebration. High over the dance floor, Rish had launched a small drone to capture the scene, and Satnam closed his eyes, imagining the bird's-eye view. How jubilant they all must have looked! He clapped along and spoke with guests as they came to congratulate him. "What a great party," they yelled over the music. "You must be so proud!" He nodded that he was; he could not recall a time that he felt so full of love and life.

Although he thought of himself as a spiritual man and had mostly given up drinking, he wanted to mark the occasion, to make a toast to his son's happiness, so he went to the bar to order the party's signature drink, the Mumbai mule.

It was there that he saw Jessie Bhatti, standing in a circle of young men all chanting "Shots, shots, shots." Satnam hadn't seen Jessie since Gobind's accident and wondered why he was there. As far as Satnam was concerned, the police's attempt to link Gobind to Jessie was a stain on their family's honour. Last month, when there'd been a stabbing in the parking lot of Goldie's Palace, news of the incident had triggered memories of Gobind's accident and stirred Satnam's fear. And now here it was, the past made present. Why was Jessie here? Who had invited him? Satnam downed his drink in one go and asked him as much.

"What's it to you?"

Satnam could tell by the way Jessie leaned forward, by his slow-motion words, that he was drunk. "It's my son's wedding," Satnam said, chin up. He would not be robbed of his izzat. He would not be disrespected at his own party.

"Right, congrats," Jessie said, and turned back to his friends.

"Gobind is my son," Satnam said, tapping him on the back. "Don't you remember me? I warned you to stay away from my family."

"You warned me?" Jessie turned around slowly, but before he could step forward, Jot got between them.

"It's okay, Uncle. I invited him. He's a friend of mine."

Satnam nodded. "Gurjot . . . you should get better friends."

"Don't pay him any attention, Uncle. He's just had one too many," Jot said, shooting Jessie a look. *Chill*, he mouthed.

Jessie folded his hands, showing due deference. "Sorry, Uncleji, I meant no disrespect."

"You okay, Dad?" It was Gobind asking.

"Fine, Son. I just don't want any trouble here," he said, referring to Jessie, who in turn raised his glass to Gobind.

"There won't be, Uncleji," Jessie said, reassuring him. "I've been friends with Jot and Devi for a long time. I'm just here to have a good time."

As Satnam walked away, he heard Gobind and Jessie exchange words; he did not know exactly what was said, only that Baby came over to intervene and, soon after, Jessie and his friends left the party.

At the moment of their departure, Satnam felt a physical relief; everyone would be safe. All he ever wanted to do was to protect his family, but from what, he had never been sure. And as for how, he was even less sure.

Perhaps Devi's grandmother, Darshan, had seen the altercation, or maybe she could read his expression, because she came over to console him the way a mother would. "Don't worry, our two great families are one now. Together we are strong and nothing can hurt us."

THE MORNING AFTER

THE LAST THING BABY REMEMBERED ABOUT THE RECEPTION WAS DEVI and him being hoisted in the air on their friends' shoulders. Riding high above the crowd, they'd been paraded around the dance floor while guests cheered and beat their glow sticks to the bhangra techno mash-up. Even when his eyes were closed, Baby could see the strobe lights pulse behind his lids, and once he'd dismounted, the blast and glow took over and now shrouded his memory in flashbulb moments. He remembered the bar lined with shots, the I-love-you-man big talk, the hands in the air waving like they just don't care, the windmills and back spins. Piecing it all together, he thought there may have been a dance-off but he couldn't be sure. Everything was a blur, the way it is when a drunk buzz settles in and softens the corners, dampens the sound and rounds out the vowels.

Rolling over in the hotel bed, he reached for Devi. Her cheek was drool damp and her face and pillow were smeared with last night's makeup, one of her eyelash strips dangling off her lid. On the nightstand next to her was a bottle of champagne in a silver ice bucket, along with a McDonald's bag and drink carrier. He didn't remember going to McDonald's but it seemed likely, given that it was their usual post-nightclub ritual. He smiled at the thought of them unrolling the limo's tinted window to order at the drive-through—or maybe they'd even stood up and popped their heads out of the sunroof as they shouted their orders. If only he remembered.

He reached across Devi's almost-naked sleeping body and slurped last night's soda through the disintegrating paper straw. Still parched, he got out of bed, downed a bottle of water from the mini-bar and popped a few pills to stop the pulsing in the back of his head. He hadn't meant to get drunk but seeing Jessie at the wedding had set him off, and it had taken everything he had to not tear into the guy. In private, Gobind had passed Baby a flask and reminded him that making a scene would only substantiate the rumours and give people more to talk about. "I'll handle it," he'd said. All of that plus the stress of the doli had taken its toll. Devi had promised they'd install a ramp alongside their front steps for Gobind, yet when Baby and his entourage of groomsmen and family arrived to collect his bride after the wedding ceremony—as was tradition—there was no ramp at the house. Gobi had said it was no big deal and that he'd just wait outside with Sonia, but Baby had refused to go in without his brother. After forty-five minutes, three rounds of limo shots and some persuading, Baby had passed his decorative sword—in a hold-my-beer kind of way—to Sonia, and he and his groomsmen, still in their silk and embroidered finery, had carried Gobind up the eight stone steps. Gobi had tried to be chill about it, even though being carried in front of a group of gawking onlookers and being made the centre of attention, especially in this way, made him visibly uncomfortable. It was one thing for them to have forgotten to make the accommodation, but then, for Gobind to have no choice but to be made a spectacle was a show of disrespect for his family that Baby could not easily forgive. To show his displeasure, he'd refused to play the traditional front door games, in which Devi's friends and female cousins would extort money from him before he'd be allowed entry to the family home to collect her. Instead, he'd simply dropped a thousand dollars on the doormat and pushed his way through the crowd of young women.

After the bride's histrionic departing ritual, when her family wept and wailed, acting as if they'd never see her again, Devi was inconsolable, crying the entire way back to Baby's family home. When Baby asked her why she was so upset, she told him she wasn't sure, only that she'd miss them. "Miss them? For real?" he said. "For as long as I've known you all you've ever wanted was to get away from them." As he said it, he realized it was the meanest thing he'd ever said to her. He wished he could take it back.

Baby crossed the room and pulled back the curtains. Outside, the sky was layered in steely cloud and slivered blue, the morning sun cutting a patchwork of light and dark across the inlet dotted with boats. He glanced over at Devi, who had groaned and pulled a pillow over her face, her free hand gesturing for him to shut the curtains as she turned away. "Too bright," she mumbled. He dropped his hands from the curtain and returned the room to its gloomy state. With their clothes tossed on the floor—and Devi's lehenga skirt, with all its layered crinolines, draped on the couch—he could imagine the haste with which they'd undressed, dropping their clothes where they'd stood, kicking off shoes before crashing into bed. He suspected they'd been too drunk to have done anything but fall asleep. Devi was usually a happy drunk, but if she mixed her liquor she'd get weepy and he'd have to reassure her that he loved her in just the right way, with just the right words, to keep her settled. Gobind had called her a tripwire drunk. "Wrong move, and boom," he'd said, the first time he'd seen her blasted.

Anticipating that Devi would be hungover too, he started the coffee and then called Gobind to see how the rest of the night went.

"Did I wake you?" Baby asked, slipping into the bathroom so as not to disturb Devi.

"No, I'm up. Though to be honest, I didn't expect to hear from you this morning. Thought you'd be busy."

"Speaking of busy . . . Is Sonia with you?"

"No. Why would she be?"

"Bro, I'm not blind—plus we share a wall, remember."

"Why didn't you say anything?"

"Figured you'd tell me if it was important." Baby heard shouting in the background. "What's going on?"

"Fucking-drama-central around here today. Turns out Mom and Boston Auntie found out about us and got into it."

"Shit, I thought they'd be thrilled."

"Yeah, not so much."

"That sucks. What are you going to do?"

"Nothing. I mean, if they aren't happy, that's on them. We want to give this a try, see where things go, you know?"

"That's awesome bro, I'm happy for you. And whatever happens, I've got you," he said, now remembering that he'd seen Gobind arguing with Jessie at the reception. Jessie had shown up late and with an entourage, after having been asked by Gobind not to come. Baby, already wasted and not wanting to get into it, had avoided Jessie almost all night. He wanted to forget about

Vegas and the rumours and just move on with life. He wanted to believe that now that he was married, he and Devi could have the life they'd planned on having before the planning had taken over their lives. He knew that calling Jessie out would only make things worse for Devi's reputation, which was now also his and his family's reputation, so he'd stood down, but when he saw Jessie shouting at Gobind he'd walked over to intervene. They both said it was nothing, but he could tell Gobind had said something to Jessie about his being there. "Not cool," was the only thing he'd heard, but it was enough to make Jessie leave.

Before leaving, Jessie had extended his hand toward Baby. "No hard feelings, eh?" Gobind wheeled forward, wedging himself between Jessie and Baby. Baby's brother had always had his back, and now it was his turn to do the same.

"Thanks man, I should probably go and help Sonia calm them down. See you tonight at Devi's?"

"Yeah, six o'clock," he said as he went back into the bedroom.

"Who were you talking to? What time is it?" Devi pulled the sheet up over her chest and twisted toward the nightstand in search of her phone, her stacked wedding bracelets jingling with every movement.

"It's ten thirty." Baby offered her a cup of coffee. "I was just checking in with Gobi."

"Is he as hungover as we are?" She took a sip and almost spat it out. "That's awful."

"It said Starbucks on it." He pointed to the in-room coffee maker. "Nah, Gobi's good. Really good actually. He and Sonia . . . they're together."

She sat straight up. "Like *together* together?"

"Yeah, seems pretty serious too."

"I knew it!" she yelled, arm raised in the air. "Details, please."

"I'll let them fill you in. They'll be at your parents' house tonight."

"Wish we didn't have to go," she said, pulling him close. "I'd rather stay here and have a wedding night do-over."

"Me too." He pulled off the fake eyelash that had strayed off her lid and onto her cheek and handed it to her. "Make a wish," he said, and kissed her.

She pushed him away and pulled off her other lash strip. "I wish for coffee, the good stuff from the place around the corner," she said, making prayer hands.

"Happy wife, happy life." He patted his tuxedo jacket for his wallet. "Anything else?"

"Yogourt, if they have it."

AFTER HE LEFT, DEVI SANK BACK INTO THE DOWN PILLOWS, STRETCHING her arms over her head before reaching for her phone and scrolling through guests' tagged wedding photos and videos. She was glad for the posts and reels; it would be weeks before Rish would have the proofs for them, and she needed to relive it straight away and from every vantage point. She wanted to see all the parts she'd missed—Baby arriving in the baraat on a decorated horse, his yellow maiyan face from the night before, her parents greeting each other in the milini, the drunkle dancing with the glass of Scotch balanced on his head, the guest selfies and the plethora of boozy boomerangs. As she scrolled through the photos, she realized how ridiculous she'd been for running away. Everyone was right, it was just cold feet.

Everything had gone according to plan, with the exception of Baby's drinking. It wasn't like him to get that way, and the fact that she'd never had to monitor his drinking or police his behaviour—the way her mother had done with her father—was one of the things she loved most about him. She knew his drinking was on account of Jessie showing up. Even though she'd assured him all along that it was all just a rumour, she suspected he knew the truth and it broke her heart in ways she hadn't imagined. Even she had drunk too much. Whole parts of the evening were missing from her memory; when she'd laid down last night, she'd had the spins and felt like she was the swirly sky in van Gogh's *Starry Night*. She remembered crying and Baby consoling her. She hoped she hadn't done anything too foolish. She'd been livid that Jessie was at the party and had tried to keep drunk Baby away from him. Jessie hadn't replied to her texts but she wished he would've respected her enough to stay away. She'd wanted to leave him as a regret, and—maybe eventually— a middle-aged what-if, but there he was at her wedding reception, her brother's so-called friend, standing in a bro circle drinking rum and coke just like the rest of them. How foolish she'd been. He was just an aging fuckboy. There was nothing special about him; Baby was the love of her life. She was glad she didn't take Dear Auntie's advice, and she was glad she listened to Jag. Telling Baby could have ruined everything.

She placed her left hand against the crisp white sheets, tilting it until the five-carat diamond caught a sliver of light, sparkling for the perfect morning post. She captioned it *Woke up a Mrs.* and tagged Baby.

Slipping on a hotel robe, Devi pulled back the curtains, grabbed a black bin and set about clearing the nightstands, tossing out the previous night's fast food and empties. When she was a child, she used to follow the Clean and Tidy maids around the house and watch how, in just a few hours, they could clear a mess away as if it had never happened. After one of her father's rages, they'd wordlessly swept up broken glass like it was nothing. From them, she'd learned how to stack dirty dishes in a dishwasher, how to remove hard water stains on glass, how to sort dirty laundry, how to scrub, polish, shine, order and how to put everything in its place to make it new and good. To her, they were magicians. When she didn't know where to start on any given day, she started by cleaning.

When she was done tidying, she picked up their wedding clothes, zipping them into their black garment bags before laying them side by side. She stared at them in their bags for a moment before picking up the extra pillows and tossing them on the bed.

"You know they have people to do that," Baby said as he came in.

"I know," she said, fluffing the pillows before joining him at the table in front of the floor-to-ceiling window.

"They didn't have the yogourt you liked, so I got this parfait thing," he said, unpacking the brown bag. "Cheers." He held his coffee cup up to hers and didn't even complain when she asked him if they could do it again so she could post it.

"To us," she said and took a small sip. "We did it."

They exchanged a quick smile and stared out at the harbour-front view as though it were a starting line. As if everything before—all the courtship, all the preparations, all the arguments—had just been about getting them to this moment, when they could begin again.

"It's something, isn't it?" Devi said, breaking the silence. She'd always hated the quiet, the way it could make a person disappear. "The view, that is."

"Sure is."

She nodded and took another sip of her coffee, aware that he was thinking about something. That his small words were placeholders.

"Last night. At the party. If I said or did anything that was out of line, I'm sorry," he said, looking down at the floor for a moment before glancing at her. "I know I drank way too much."

She smiled at him and reached for his hand. "It's fine. You were fine."

"Really?" His face softened.

"Yeah," she said, surprising herself. "I mean, everyone was a little drunk, including me. I just hope they didn't get anything too embarrassing on camera." She knew that by the time they saw the wedding video, Rish would have sanitized their remembrance, editing out all the questionable moments and showing them only what they wanted to look back on, so that years later when they rewatched it they'd both see how happy they'd been. "It's totally fine," she reassured him once more. "Besides, it's me that owes you an apology. These last weeks leading up to the wedding, I kind of lost myself in all of it. You know I'd never intentionally do anything to hurt you, right?" she said, knowing that this was the one true thing she could say. She hadn't set out to hurt him.

"I know," he said, holding her gaze in a way that suggested he did know. He knew everything.

Unsure of what to say next, she returned her gaze to the water, to what was in front of them. She wondered if marriage had already changed her. Unmarried Devi would have blasted him for being drunk. She would have blamed him for all her bad behaviour. She would have mapped out a timeline of wrongdoings with inciting events and fault lines that all led back to him. She would manage to cast herself as victim and him as villain. They would have fought about it. She would have demanded accountability and resisted responsibility the way she never saw her mother do. And yet here she was, settling for a vague apology and offering one in return. And much to her surprise, he accepted it. He accepted her.

For weeks she'd questioned why she was settling down—or settling for, as if marrying Baby was a lesser possibility than all her future propositions; yet, as she looked at him staring at the horizon, she realized it had never been about that. There was a distinction that she hadn't understood before, and was only now becoming clear. It was not a settling for, but a settling with.

EPILOGUE

A COMMUNITY IN CRISIS

Priya Deol, *Awaaz*

Jessie Bhatti was gunned down in his family home in Punjab, India, on October 18, 2022. Though local police suspect a botched home invasion, the RCMP, who are working in partnership with the Indian authorities, say they have yet to rule out whether Bhatti's killing could be tied to local ongoing gang activity. The victim, who was known to police, was in India visiting his family. This brutal killing is just another in a string of murders and shootings that have left families shattered and a community in crisis.

ENGAGEMENT ANNOUNCEMENT

Priya Deol, *Awaaz*

Satnam Singh Atwal and Balbir Kaur Atwal are pleased to announce the engagement of their son Gobind Singh Atwal to Sonia Kaur Nijjar, daughter of Dr. Gurmaan Singh Nijjar and Dr. Veero Kaur Nijjar. The couple plans to marry next summer in Boston, Massachusetts, where the bride's family resides.

ACKNOWLEDGEMENTS

THANKS FIRST AND ALWAYS TO SAT, AMIT AND ARUN FOR YOUR unwavering love, support and encouragement. To Xena, my faithful companion, for keeping me company throughout the creative process. Thanks to Nin, Kay and Subby for being discerning first readers, fans and subject matter experts and enthusiasts. A shout-out to Mira, whose insightful editorial feedback unlocked new chapters. Thanks to my agent at Westwood Creative Artists, John Pearce, who loved the idea and structure of this book from the start. Thanks to my editor, Karlene Nicolajsen, my copy editor, Emma Skagen, and the entire team at Douglas & McIntyre for your expertise. Much love to my family and friends who make everything seem possible.

Photo by Karolina Turek

GURJINDER BASRAN is the award-winning author of three previous works of fiction. Her debut novel, *Everything Was Good-bye*, was the recipient of the Ethel Wilson Fiction Prize and her work regularly appears on must-read lists. She lives in Delta, BC with her family.